The King's Fool

Mahi Binebine

The King's Fool

Translated from the French by
Ben Faccini

MACLEHOSE PRESS
QUERCUS · LONDON

First published as *Le Fou du roi* by Editions Stock, Paris, in 2017

First published in Great Britain in 2020 by MacLehose Press

This paperback edition published in 2022 by

MacLehose Press
An imprint of Quercus Publishing Ltd
Carmelite House
50 Victoria Embankment
London EC4Y 0DZ

An Hachette UK company

This book is supported by the Institut français (Royaume-Uni)
as part of the Burgess programme.

ROYAUME-UNI

A CIP catalogue record for this book is available from the British Library.

ISBN (MMP) 978 0 85705 824 9
ISBN (Ebook) 978 0 85705 823 2

2 4 6 8 10 9 7 5 3 1

Designed and typeset in Bembo by Patty Rennie
Printed and bound in Great Britain by Clays Ltd, Elcograf S.p.A.

MIX
Paper from
responsible sources
FSC® C104740

For Papa

Poor clown! What endless, impossible pain there is in the merriment of the buffoon! What a dreadful job laughter is!

VICTOR HUGO, *Choses vues*

EVERYTHING SEEMED NORMAL, BUT it was not. A moonless night, embroidered with pale stars, cloaked two figures in the vast courtyard of the palace. Sidi moved slowly along paths dotted with lanterns, bordered by trees – orange, almond, doum palms. I kept close, slightly bowed, a touch obsequious, as required when escorting the king. Night-flowering jasmine infused the humid July air. Sidi held his aching belly with both hands, letting out occasional groans. The invisible beast gnawing at his bowels barely gave him a moment's respite, and he was finding it harder to stand up straight. It was painful to watch him suffer, but I refrained from showing it. I forced myself to crack a few jokes – that was my job, to make my master laugh. Sidi was not in the mood. He scarcely listened, his face a knot of wrinkles which looked as if they had grown deeper all at once.

Everything seemed normal, but nothing is normal when the lion is on its knees and its claws have become useless splinters of wood; when the dying fire in its eyes inspires more pity than fear; when its gaze has turned inwards to the depths of its defeated body; when the roars of yester-day are no more than faint echoes of a life burned at both ends, heavy with every kind of excess: bitter regrets, un-acknowledged defeats, resounding half-victories, great joys and sorrows, sacrifices and misgivings, too – a tumult through which angels and demons dance to the Grim Reaper's tune.

Everything seemed normal, but I could feel a tightness in my chest. I prayed, day and night, that God would free my master of his illness and, if needed, inflict me with it on his behalf. I was willing to take on his sickness, the spasms in his guts, the shooting pain in his sides. Had I not been the king's devoted servant for thirty-five years, his enduringly resource-ful entertainer, his appointed theologian – despite his role as Commander of the Faithful? His literary consultant, too: his only fount of knowledge when it came to the dazzling world of poetry, a witness to the days when the Arabs waged war in verse, when grammarians argued for months about into-nation and declensions, about a trifling accent; an era when mathematical and astrological equations were the closest we came to religion . . . blissful times that now felt as though they had never existed.

Everything seemed normal, but your humble servant knew otherwise. I, Mohamed ben Mohamed – the scum of Marrakesh's rancid effluence, the least likely man ever to have rubbed shoulders with the elite, an escapee from the deepest sewers of humanity – I was there on that July evening, a few steps behind my moribund master, my head still reverberat-ing with the doctor's dire verdict: "In two or three days we'll all be orphans."

Sidi's attention was grabbed by an unusual light in the gift room: a vast storeroom where thousands of presents, the residue of the king's innumerable parties, were piled up, still in their original wrapping paper.

"Come," the king said. "Let's go and see what's up."

"It's late, Sidi. The night is chilly. We should go back."

"Not before I catch the fiend who's robbing me before I'm even in my grave," he grumbled, pushing ahead.

"Someone must be cleaning, Sidi, that's all."

"At this time of night?"

I didn't reply. The king seemed bent on getting to the bottom of the matter.

When you walk through the palace at night, you would be wrong to imagine that you are alone. Dozens of spying eyes follow you, watching your every move. I know what I'm talking about. For decades, I've lived behind these walls glinting with mosaics, in these gardens studded with fountains that gurgle the same song at each twist in the path. It seemed incredible to me that someone would be foolish enough to steal from the very heart of the royal household. Yet we all knew the king was a shadow of his former self, and as a result some presumed they had the right to attempt the most foolish things.

We limped our way towards the northern wing of the palace, climbed some steps, headed down a long, vaulted corridor only used by the staff and saw the door to Ali Baba's cave ajar. Sidi gave it a gentle nudge, peered through the gap and stood still. Then he silently set foot inside. I slipped in behind him. The scene that met our eyes was enlightening to say the least, and would have been unthinkable only weeks previously. The hem of his djellaba held up to form a bundle, an old slave was busy scooping up precious caskets, felt-lined coffers and objects of all kinds. He must have been hard of hearing not to have noticed our arrival, but when Sidi cleared his throat, the man spun round and nearly passed out at the sight of the king standing right there before him. Petrified, shaking, the slave appeared to be trying to speak, yet no sound would leave his mouth. His ebony skin turned purple, its shininess exaggerated by the sweat streaming down his forehead in a sheen of terror. Given Sidi's reputation, I didn't give the brazen idiot much of a chance. If he was lucky, the fearsome fire slaves in charge of punishments would send him packing with a hundred lashes. Proper whips, too, made from plaited oxtail, dipped in ice-cold water. One crack of these whips was retribution enough. I didn't dare think of the alternative. But the king was unpredictable. No-one could guess how he would react. He could crush a man for a trifle just as he could forgive the most serious of offences.

We had further proof of it that evening.

"Hurry up," he said to the thief. "Get on with it, and scarper! If the guards catch you, you'll end up with a noose around your neck."

The slave did not know which way to turn, unsure whether to believe his master or not. As he remained rooted to the spot, I leaned over, rummaged through his upturned djellaba, removed what seemed to be an expensive watch case and slipped it into my hood.

"At least have the decency to share some of your spoils, fat arse. Now get a move on before Sidi changes his mind!"

Noticing the beginnings of a smile on my master's weary

face, I added, "Consider yourself lucky that Sidi's in a good mood this evening. As a matter of fact, if I were you, I'd ask him for another favour."

The slave stared at me in disbelief. The king had begun to smile now.

"I don't know. Request a transport licence of some kind," I said. "A franchise to sustain you in your dotage?"

"What kind of franchise?" The king chuckled.

I leaned towards the slave and whispered, "A railway franchise."

"A railway franchise, Your Majesty," the poor man stuttered.

The king guffawed, reawakening the pain in his sides, but it didn't stop him. He laughed on and it was as if a cloud of butterflies had taken flight.

"I think an airline franchise might suit our man better," I said, grinning. Then I turned to the slave. "Go on, get out of here, you've earned your treasure."

We watched him stagger away, a trickle of urine in his wake.

Sidi remained a while longer in that vast storeroom weighed down by a mountain of gifts he had never had the time nor the inclination to unwrap. This abundance brought him no pleasure at all. We both knew he had no need for any of it where he was heading. Letting the slave walk free, however, had cheered him no end.

"Come," he said, his voice calm. "Let's go."

2

EVERYONE IN THE ROYAL palace had been pretending for weeks. A heaviness had replaced the usual hustle and bustle. Silence swept through every courtyard, down every corridor, into the drawing-rooms and kitchens. Only muffled echoes and whisperings escaped here and there. The guards' loud footsteps had once reassured us, but now they tiptoed about. The slaves who used to proclaim "Long life to His Majesty" at every possible opportunity had also fallen quiet. The constant toing and froing of high-ranking officials and ministers did not bode well – and nor did the presence of the crown prince and other members of the royal family. They, too, were pretending. Just like the muezzin of the palace mosque, whose melancholic voice had been drowned out by his shriller colleagues in town. Sitting at table, we did our best to eat, to talk as we always had, to comment on the escalating violence in the daily news, to laugh about this and that.

Sidi's favourite granddaughter, Sofia, was far more skilled at eliciting a smile from him than I. She regularly stole my limelight, shamelessly stepped on my toes. I'm embarrassed to admit it, but even at the age of seventy, I was often jealous of the snickering, carefree little blonde child. I'd catch the king staring at her pink cheeks and bouncy, golden hair, her hazelnut eyes nearly swallowed by her spoiled pout. "My snowy pearl," he'd say, his face aglow, marvelling the way only a dark-skinned Bedouin could marvel at an alien, Northern beauty like hers. To him, she was a miracle, this child with milky-white skin, who at the age of eight already spoke the strange languages of her many governesses, a confusion that went straight over my head. She and I fought with ill-matched weapons. I deployed all the tricks I could muster to counter her ability to charm my master, and he took a wicked delight in this secret rivalry. Luckily, I am not one to give up on things. I've walked the back corridors of power long enough to know the codes and the myriad tactics required to survive. I've always had to compete to earn my crust. I wasn't going to be unseated by a snotty-nosed brat like her.

No, I did not like Sofia. But in the palace, as elsewhere, royal blood remained sacred. So I just smiled like everyone else and extolled the remarkable qualities the Heavens had conferred on His Majesty's angel: her beauty, first and foremost; her playfulness, too; her startling sense of humour and intelligence, of course, and the sort of brains the Good Lord, in His great mercy, only ever grants the blue-blooded. What a hypocrite, I hear you say. Of course, but I was no different from the rest of the flies swarming about that noble household.

The evenings, however, were mine and mine alone. As soon as the little terror had gone to bed, I had my master to myself and I was, once more, the centre of his world. He looked at me in admiration, gladly listened and waited for me to come up with a bon mot, a subtle gibe, maybe a scholarly parallel between a contemporary affair and one that had occurred in the days of the Umayyad Caliphate. I would sprinkle my conversation with juicy anecdotes, twists and a dose of jeopardy. I would give free rein to my fantasies, catch up on the time I'd lost to the blonde whippersnapper that day. Rid of her poisonous meddling, back in the comfort of my official role, I embraced artifice, but did my darnedest to make it sound plausible. I melded reality and fiction, let myself be carried along as if in a daydream. I became the magician again, a unique being whom no-one other than the king could afford to employ. I pulled forgotten lives from my hat, stories that had been languishing in my head and the clouds above: wondrous tales crafted with meticulous words and elaborate imagery, teased to life by my poetic musings, picked by my trembling hand and fashioned into a bouquet that I respectfully offered my master.

You see, the ultimate aim of my strange existence is to make the king happy. I live for that. Nothing gives me as much joy and satisfaction as seeing Sidi's face light up.

Mine is a strange fate. I, Mohamed ben Mohamed, the slum kid, was born without any particular talent other than the capacity to remember everything I hear. The Heavens endowed me with a prodigious memory, quite unlike that of any other two-legged creature: I absorb the slightest word that skims past my ears, literally everything, and I mean absolutely everything. I can still describe, in great detail, and with devilish accuracy, a superficial conversation I had with a casual acquaintance fifty years ago. As for the books I've read – and I've read quite a few – I can recite them all, down to the last comma, prefaces included. Believe it or not, God decided to bestow this startling ability on me and, while some might well call it a gift – and it is, to a certain extent – I will spare you an account of the tremendous time and energy I've had to expend to shed all the resentment I've accumulated, since I recall the bad as well as the good. Bitter, persistent grudges are the burden of those who can't forget, for there is more than an element of forgetting to forgiveness. Otherwise it's hard, if not impossible, isn't it? When you scrape at an old wound, when you jab at a particular memory, all compassion is erased. The idea of letting past grievances go, or starting afresh, is just wishful thinking. But that's a different story. I want to tell you only about the benefits of this memory of mine, and how it launched my meteoric rise to the highest echelons of power. It made me the person I am today, the foremost courtier of the mightiest man in the kingdom. I must say, without wanting to boast, that my master appreciates me a lot more than the rabble of musicians, storytellers and simpering sycophants who make up the rest of the court. I'm the scholar who draws the cleverest minds to the palace – all erudite conversations hinge around me. You see, I owe everything to this perfect recall of mine, which I instinctively knew I had to make careful use of from an early age. The study of the Qur'an, or the Hadiths as reported by the Prophet's companions, was child's play for me. Learning a thousand verses to master Arabic grammar was no sweat at all, even though my peers at the Ben Youssef Madrasa struggled. As for poetry, there isn't a single poet whose work I don't know inside out. It's just the way it is and that's that. Even if I try to free my mind of all the nonsense filling it, I can't. Nothing works. The many drawers that make up my brain snap shut the moment I pull them open, refusing to yield their contents. So, in spite of myself, I hold on to both the useful and the useless, the essential and the inessential — a curdling of information that would clog anyone else's mind, but that my head (though small in size) manages to accommodate. I only have to tug on a thread to loosen the past, to let it unravel in front of me, and it shoves the present away with all the self-importance and conceit of an ancestor bossing his descendants around. So, there you are: I wanted to make all this clear, so you understand how a man of my humble origins managed to enter a world as ruthless as the royal court and become the king's favourite.

This astonishing story is mine. I didn't choose it; I didn't try to dodge it, either. I just let things happen, like most people.

It all began with a rather unlikely friendship. Ben Brahim would not have been the kind of companion I'd normally have chosen. For a start, he was a good ten years older than me, and his marked fondness for alcohol, and handsome young men, challenged my puritanical upbringing. My sexual preferences could not have been more conventional, and the idea of not being able to control my urges disgusted me. Socialising with such an individual ran, so to speak, against my nature. All the more so as our friendship could have been misconstrued. Slander, of course, is a national sport in this country, and consorting with Ben Brahim laid me open to all sorts of gossip. But this man – and I weigh my words carefully – was without question the greatest poet our country has ever seen.

How can I tell you about the beginnings of our friendship without first mentioning my father, Mohamed, a barber by profession? He was also a musician, a storyteller and a most delightful man. There were few with his qualities, which is why he ended up working at the court of Pasha El Glaoui, who ruled over the southern part of the country at the time of the French protectorate. The pasha's role, as the occupiers' puppet, was to "pacify and civilise" whole stretches of this bountiful realm of ours. Now, to get back to our alcoholic, homosexual and penniless poet, he joined the court in order to guarantee both his financial survival and protection for his antics. Come evening, he would saunter off to bars frequented by soldiers, drink until he was paralytic, and sniff out sensitive souls willing to spend the night with him. Like some nocturnal hunter, he prowled our Muslim lands in a drunken stupor, combing the city's underworld for hidden pleasures. In exchange, he recited poems night and day to the glory of his benefactor and shield: His Excellency the pasha. I first came across Ben Brahim in the palace where my father worked as I'd often eat my meals in the kitchens – such was the master's generosity towards his servants' offspring. I was a young student and the poet's eloquence and distinction immediately intrigued me. Actually, if I'm totally honest, Ben Brahim noticed me because of the shapely buttocks with which Mother Nature had blessed me, but he quickly understood that I wasn't that way inclined. He didn't give up, though, and he carried on eyeing me up as our friendship grew – it became a source of great amusement between us. But he soon got distracted by my mind, by my uncommon ability to recite long-winded poems in one fell swoop, without a moment's hesitation. We'd prolong our conversations, walk the streets and parks of the city, and visit bars at nightfall. I loved to escort him and let myself be swept along by his rhetorical flights of fancy, imbibing his words as if they were some kind of celestial nectar. I had to run to keep up with his escapades in the real world, too, as much as my imagination would allow, and I committed every one of his utterances to memory. While Ben Brahim drank wine, I drank mint tea without sugar. A lot of wine and a lot of tea, sweetened by his colourful, flowery phrases. The more he drank, the more he recited poems from lost eras, from far-off worlds. I was the sole audience for this rush of swirling quatrains, as intricate as they were bawdy and perplexing, brimming with parody and repressed emotion. They were moments of grace, generously handed to me because, even when he was blind drunk, Ben Brahim knew I understood their meaning, that I relished his metaphors buoyed by ethereal rhythm, his images unconstrained by the tethers of language. They lifted me up and I twirled inside his mind as much as my own, the two of us, in unison. The more uninhibited he became, the more he abandoned all thought of eulogising his protector, and the fat stipend that went with his position. Instead, he sung of forbidden love in all its forms, glorifying wine and the freedom it brought us. I say "us" as this is how I shared in his drunkenness.

A sort of mercenary bond grew between us. How can I describe it without appearing to be a crook? I recalled the poems he recited during his carousing, and the next day, when he was sober in the pasha's kitchens, I sold them back to him at a premium. Ben Brahim would cough up without batting an eyelid. Sometimes I would play hard to get when I spotted a gift from the pasha on his person – a shining watch, or something similar. I would hook a snippet of a quatrain on a stick and dangle it in front of his eyes, a poem I knew off by heart, but which he'd forgotten. It was a chunk of pure gold in my memory and I could see how he was drooling all over it.

"What did I recite to you yesterday evening?" he'd ask, his eyes glistening and anxious.

"A fabulous poem! A miracle of literature . . ."

"Repeat it!"

"I'm always a little ropey at this time in the morning."

"How much?"

I tried to gauge his level of interest before setting my price.

"Five dirhams."

"I haven't got that much. I drank it all last night, as you know."

"I like your watch," I said, smiling.

"It's a gift from the pasha," he protested.

"Up to you."

I recited a few lines to reel him in:

"Poetry, I've had enough, abandon me . . . leave, turn on your heels . . . Chase those who need you most. Shower them in pain, stifle them with the agony of knowledge."

Ben Brahim removed his watch and handed it to me.

I can say today, even though I'm a little ashamed, that this man made me rich, in all senses of the word. I learned to live by observing his life – how to laugh, how to sing. I took his mischievousness as my benchmark, and found a way to outmanoeuvre my foes, to pick their flimsy arguments apart. Like him, I discovered I could shock without a twinge of remorse, grinning at the same time. One day – as he leaned on a counter in a bar, prayer beads in one hand and a glass of wine in the other – the poet was accosted by a man with a thick beard. He didn't cross the threshold of the establishment, but shouted over at Ben Brahim in an accusing voice:

"Tell me, sir, how can a man of your stature drink wine, when your knowledge of Islamic culture is recognised by all? On the day of the Last Judgement, those prayer beads you turn in your fingers will reveal to God that you drank wine!"

The poet lifted his prayer beads, stared back at the intruder and slowly dunked them in his glass. We looked at him aghast.

"These prayer beads will no doubt testify that I drank wine, but I will bear witness to the fact that they swam in it."

Many people still relish the squalid rumours about this man, who was both cursed and adored in this taboo-riddled society of ours.

Ben Brahim was an exceptional human being and, without knowing it, he altered the course of my life.

The foreign settlers ended up being driven out of the country, and the treacherous pasha who had helped overthrow a monarch years before didn't last long. His empire, which many believed would last for ever, collapsed. The good old rabble burned everything they could lay their hands on, murdering and raping as they went. The poet died humiliated, destitute, his star having dramatically fallen. His poetry, however, lived on in the memories of many, and on random scraps of paper.

Years later, I had the immense privilege of chaperoning the "Star of the East", the mythical singer Umm Kulthum, on a tour of Marrakesh, and recited reams of Ben Brahim's poetry to her. He was, after all, the "Red City's poet" and part of our heritage. His incomparable ballads had a strong effect on the diva. Here was an exceptional man who had lived in our times even though he could have shone in any century – his life the sort of gift the Heavens grant us only sparingly.

A few days into her stay, while performing for the king, the diva mentioned our illustrious poet and how a collection of his works was woefully lacking. She spoke admiringly of the artist, a man worthy of Omar Khayyam himself, and said how she would have loved to have sung and celebrated his genius. Cornered, and a little put out, the king promised to make up for this unforgivable oversight as soon as possible. The moment the singer left the country, he summoned all those who were familiar with Ben Brahim's *œuvre* and granted them access to the pasha's confiscated library, ordering them to collate the poet's works as fast as possible. It took months and I, of course, helped with the assignment.

The collection was presented to the king and he organised a sumptuous feast to honour our work. He was both pleased and vexed, however, as the poet had written numerous paeans to Pasha El Glaoui, a sworn enemy of the monarchy. At the dinner, the king turned to me, saying:

"Let me hear some satire Ben Brahim wrote about that collaborator pasha of yours."

The room fell silent.

"Your Majesty," I said, "I don't recall any such poems. There aren't any. And even if there were, I wouldn't have learned them off by heart."

"And why not?" the king asked indignantly.

"Because that man fed me and protected me as a child. He's long dead now, of course, but please don't ask me to insult his memory."

Another uncomfortable silence spread over the gathering. Knowing the king the way they did, the courtiers weren't giving me much chance of walking out of there alive. I was already on borrowed time. A ripple of protest began, but the king unexpectedly turned to the sycophants around him and said:

"Now you see, gentlemen, here is an honourable man, loyal in ways you'll never understand."

My future colleagues lowered their two-faced heads and smiled at me with precipitous sympathy. This loyalty secured me thirty-five years of service in that palace. I accompanied the king, day and night, throughout the kingdom and abroad. And now, in these sad times, with his death fast approaching, I'm still at his side.

3

IT'S EASY TO FEEL unsettled on entering the palace. A military atmosphere flows through its interminable corridors and doorways. Expressionless guards — beefcakes handpicked from the best of Africa's brawn — decked out in full regalia, and flanked by a battalion of lackeys in white burnous cloaks and red *chechia* hats, glare down at you from a great height. Harsh, synchronised voices, loud enough to give you the jitters, ring out whenever a member of the royal family walks by. Having grown up behind the scenes in the pasha's residence, my first steps in Sidi's palace didn't come as too much of a shock. In fact, accustomed to the hubbub of stately ceremonies, I felt rather at home. Yet I would have been unable to say what I was thinking on that first day. Becoming a member of the royal court might have been the ultimate ambition of many of my peers, but it certainly wasn't mine. Perhaps I wanted to emulate my father, as young people so often do, because nothing in particular predisposed or attracted me to courtly life. All forms of bowing and prostration sickened me. Besides, I thought my education and erudition had released me from bootlicking and fake pleasantries. But however keen you are to escape your fate, it always catches up with you, and sneakily nudges your life back into the narrow and unforgiving groove of your *mektoub*. Such is the way of destiny.

So I perpetuated my father's work at court and took it to new heights. An exceptional man, dressed in a white djellaba and tatty babouche slippers, he would hold my hand on Fridays, after prayers, as we proudly ambled through the back alleys of the medina. The deference with which the merchants of the souk greeted him no doubt played a part in my career choice. I loved seeing all those poor wretches crowd around us, desperate to ask my father to pass on their grievances to the pasha. Miserable brutes whose lives and deaths depended on Papa's readiness to speak to His Excellency on their behalf. Was I that enthralled by our ruling class, without realising it? A caste who hoist you so high up into the sky that mere mortals seem like insignificant ants. Did a contaminated blood run in my veins, the kind of blood that likes to prop up power-hungry men? Men who, one way or another, end up consorting with the devil? They might be ordinary to begin with, but years later they are driven to make appalling decisions, guided by a logic beyond their control. Would I become just another puppet caught up in the deadly battle between good and evil? I damned well didn't know. I entered that huge palace like a moth drawn to light. Joy and fear jostled in my mind as I took my first steps in Sidi's household. My doubts weren't too existential, however: this wasn't about metaphysics. I was pondering basic, down-to-earth, pragmatic questions: how could I fulfil my duties without too many hitches and blunders? Would I captivate or disappoint my new master? And how would I carve out a place for myself with all those old-timers clustered around the king, not just the musicians and charmers but the black dwarf called Boudda, too, apparently the only one who could get away with blurting out obscenities in front of Sidi? How could I make my mark amongst such a bunch of people already bound by ingrained codes and years of service at court? I had a choice between a quiet debut, watching my every word, not ruffling too many feathers, and a grand entrance which would single me out as a man of letters, eager to rise above the mediocrity of all the other imbeciles. In such moments, I have to confess, you feel very alone. Awfully alone. The slightest slip-up can prove fatal. Displeasing His Majesty meant immediate disgrace – and permanent disgrace, too. Which wouldn't have caused me that much pain except for the fact that I find failure intolerable – despite my father having harped on about defeat being more instructive than success. To leave on my own terms was one thing, but to be dismissed like a dog was quite another, unbearable to the cocky, award-winning student of the Ben Youssef Madrasa that I was. Over the course of my short life, I'd already had to face many difficulties, and had fought hard to claim a share of the elevated world to which I felt entitled. And rightly so, I believed. Step by step, story by story, poem by poem, with all the wisdom I'd garnered, I'd built and climbed my own staircase. Astonishingly, I'd managed to convince my father that I shouldn't take on his barbershop. Such a victory might seem rather pathetic to some, lacklustre to say the least, but to persuade my father – who cut hair, set bones and cured all sorts of ills for a living – that words could sustain a man was nothing short of a miracle. Papa still insisted I worked at the barbershop until closing time after my lessons at the madrasa. I spent many an hour fiddling with greasy, lice-ridden hair, healing wounds, resetting bones, positioning bamboo sticks around fractures, all sound drowned out by screeches of pain – even distracting boys with imaginary birds as they had their foreskins lopped off, little yelling cherubs who regularly fainted on the spot.

I did not feel alone as I entered the palace that evening. My friend Ben Brahim held my hand. His invisible presence reassured me as I walked towards my destiny. The poet's spirits took possession of my emotions, quelled my fears and doubts, calmed my quivering voice and shaky hands, and urged me to strut past the hostile stares. I was clearly a threat, a potential barrier between the courtiers and their master's love. A dozen pairs of eyes stared at me, assessed the quality of my djellaba, the felt of the tarboosh on my head, the suppleness of the leather on the babouche slippers my father had given me. Ben Brahim came to my rescue at the first attack. The words I used were his. I had just sat down on the blue velvet sofa of the vast sitting room when the dwarf heckled me:

"Is it true, Mohamed, that the people of Marrakesh . . ."

"Forgive me, my little friend," I replied. "You should learn to speak like a grown-up. You say 'Fqih' Mohamed when addressing a man of my rank and culture."

The king smiled and said:

"Everyone, please welcome Fqih Mohamed to our household."

Or just "the Fqih" – as I became known from then on. I was not merely another hireling in the royal palace, but a scholar and a master in the king's service. In thirty seconds flat, I'd achieved the status required for my role. Jester, for sure, though not any old clown whatever the circumstances. My position as an intellectual had been acknowledged by the whole court, by order of His Majesty.

That said, people from Marrakesh loathe all forms of conflict. They hate confrontation. They are a cheery, jocular bunch, and partygoers to boot. I was no exception. I quickly learned to keep my opinions in check and mocked the arrogance of scholars, deathly dull people who love the sound of their own voices – their encyclopaedic knowledge of no interest to anyone but themselves. Fickleness became second nature as I trained to be a courtier.

Before winning the king's heart, I undertook, on my father's shrewd advice, to charm those around him. It was far from a foregone conclusion that I would succeed. Each courtier came from a different background, region and culture: it was extremely hard to get on with one without offending another. All the more so as their characters could morph from one minute to the next, mutating like chameleons to match the king's moods. It was impossible to assess their thoughts with any accuracy, such was their irrepressible and insatiable desire to please Sidi. Make no mistake: everything I accused my colleagues of would later apply to me. I just wasn't aware of it at the time.

I started by getting close to the most affable of all the courtiers: a musician named Saher. An upright, congenial man, whose vulnerability was, ironically, his best protection – he was such easy prey that the carnivorous animals at the top of the court food chain could have eaten him alive. Yet no-one picked on him because he posed no threat. On the contrary, he flattered the various courtiers' egos as if they, too, were of royal blood – to the point where the king could have taken offence, but he never did. Saher was an extraordinary oud player, blessed with a gentle, broken voice. There was an otherworldliness to him: he lived in a bubble all of his own, brimming with dreams, poetry and music. His favourite artists, Middle Eastern poets, composers and singers, were geniuses from the last century, people I also held in high regard. It didn't require much effort, therefore, to win him over. Our friendship lasted decades.

We would gather in an exceedingly comfortable sitting room near the king's private quarters and wait for the evening summons. The antechamber was draped in an emerald-green velvet, with religious texts embroidered in gold, and a pattern of arches that seemed to invite you in, as if to a mysterious realm reserved for the lucky few. Calmness reigned in that room. It was like a still river before the rush of a flood, even though the worst manifestations of human wickedness were devised there: outrageous schemes, weaselly plots, perverse machinations and a thousand other treacheries that could make or break careers and lives, open the doors of paradise to hell, and vice versa – a place where prestigious titles and ranks were stripped away, where ministers and slaves became interchangeable and everything depended on who stood nearest to the royal light.

When the melodious but stern voice of a minder called us, we all jumped up as one and headed to Sidi's quarters, chirpy and sprightly, each of us hoarding a succulent morsel of a story in our satchels, an individually crafted and jealously kept secret to offer His Majesty. The race was on to see which one of us would extract the first smile from Sidi. Without wanting to brag, I have to say that I was streets ahead of my colleagues, even though I planned nothing in advance. I would improvise on the spot, relying on circumstances to guide me. As my colleagues exhausted themselves, adjusting their ready-made stories to the situation at hand, I'd already drawn my gun and peppered the room with hilarious, scathing quips. And if the king laughed, the fools had to laugh with him, concealing their resentment behind their smiles. Such were our daily battles in His Most Gracious Majesty's inner sanctum. A sanctuary that was organised like the public square of a medina. Sitting cross-legged on thick carpets, we bunched together according to our skills, acting out a charade of the everyday city life Sidi would never know. Some played Tarot-like cards and hurled surprisingly lewd insults at their opponents; others huddled round Saher to hear his exquisitely monotonous chants. Onlookers encouraged Boudda the dwarf's ridiculous rantings; a few gasped in disbelief at yet another of the fortune-teller Bilal's predictions or applauded Moussa the herbalist's improbable recipes . . . It was like a miniature court of miracles, with Sidi sprawled out on a sofa, a book in one hand and prayer beads in the other, vaguely following events from the corner of his eye. Nothing eluded him. He knew exactly who had cheated at cards (it wasn't hard to guess as it was often yours truly), and he chuckled at the dwarf's dishonesty without ever taking him to task, rocking his head back and forth when Saher plucked a previously unheard piece from the depths of his soul or from some ancient, forgotten repertoire.

So this was how we kept ourselves and the master busy until dawn prayers, striving to help him forget the worries of his long day, distracting him with crazy and unexpected tricks, attempting to transform that place of great solemnity and decision-making into an oasis of calm.

From time to time, the evening summons would be delayed, or not take place at all. Then the waiting would drag on for hours, all night even. The chamberlain only sent us home once he was quite sure Sidi was fast asleep. We often remained pent up in the royal antechamber, killing time as best we could. I would read, devouring anything I could lay my hands on, or play cards, refusing to give in to the temptation of the *maajoun* cakes which were handed around under the table: a mix of honey, almonds, walnuts and the best hashish from Ketama, an absolute delight provided you didn't stint on the ingredients. They turned the endless waiting into flashes of wonder. I knew the curiously mystical virtues of these cakes, having gorged on them on numerous occasions, but I no longer relied on them, unlike many of my colleagues. So there we were, Sidi's motley crew, bound by intense friendships – and riven by entrenched hatreds, too. Aside from Dr Mourra, Saher was the only member of our group to have earned unanimous approval. He never had a harsh word for anyone, never gave anyone a dirty look. He smiled without fail even in moments of sadness, and those occasions were as readable on his face as the lines of a book. Hidden behind his oud and his thick glasses, you would see him begin to soar, as if carried by the wings of his melody and nothing could hold him back. His shyness vanished in an instant and his head moved, in sync with the tune, as if he were taming the surge of notes lest they be tempted by disorder. He floated on invisible clouds, danced with spirits of light that only he could see, and then pulled back in pain, on the cusp of tears, when the love story he was singing ended badly. Saher was my first true friend at the king's court. He remained close to me, but died too soon, as happens so often with the best of men. We shared an unadulterated love of poetry and music and we would exhaust ourselves discussing the riotous lives of poets, right down to the circumstances in which they had composed their work, and the constraints of their times . . . Later I'll tell you his story. It's as splendid as it is heart-rending. That's the way things go in our part of the world.

My second conquest was Dr Mourra. Sidi was a hypochondriac, and this courageous man had to remain within a hundred-metre radius of the king at all times. It was a life sentence, without the chance of parole. No matter the weather, night or day, Dr Mourra was there, within easy reach of our master. I can assure you that with a single glance, with an eye that stripped you naked and probed deep inside your body, this magician could pinpoint your medical history – your father's and grandfather's, too. Yet this venerated man was the unhappiest of us all, a victim of his own remarkable skills.

33

"When you hire your arse out you don't sit on it," my mother would have said. And Dr Mourra's arse was contracted for life. While the rest of us could bunk off for the odd day during the holiday season, he could not. The mere thought of his absence brought the monarch out in hives, so Sidi had ended up sequestering the man's whole family within the palace walls. Dr Mourra had grown up in a village outside Marrakesh and we found we had an immediate regional kinship. Our mutual singsong accent, shared by the people of the South, quickly brought us together. Small, stocky, with a large paunch, with even less hair on his head than me, and of rather austere appearance, he was one of those people who looked as though they have been born old. It was hard to imagine him as a child tugging at the hem of his mother's djellaba. He tried to shake off this persistent image by telling us supposedly funny stories, but he never managed to be entertaining. His explanations were so long-winded, so thoroughly reasoned, that you forgot the opening gambit. We laughed more at the mess he made of telling jokes than at the jokes themselves. Dr Mourra didn't seem to mind and laughed heartily with us. He was a decent fellow, and from a young age he'd always behaved with the utmost regard for others, his life devoted to perfecting everything he undertook. To be the best in his field was his ultimate goal, his *raison d'être*, his religion. The richly deserved scholarship the French colonisers awarded him (rarely given to natives) meant that, come independence, he was the only professor of medicine in the whole country. A prominence which led him (or rather condemned him, as we've seen) straight to a life in the royal palace. Of humble birth, Dr Mourra had to fight hard to find his rightful place at court. He had only his expertise to rely on – and it wasn't always enough. So he flaunted what he had, sold his soul to the devil, gambled his dignity away and ended up, like the rest of us, engulfed by the blaze of an unknowable sun, blinded by the irresistible light of power. From then on, whims, delusions, obsessions and fears became his daily lot. Dr Mourra watched over His Majesty like no-one else. He knew how to allay his fears, how to keep his demons in check, even with a permanent Sword of Damocles over his head. Bearing ultimate responsibility for a monarch's health must be one of the worst curses, something you wouldn't wish on any living creature. "When the Good Lord wants to punish an ant," my mother would have again said, "he gives it the gift of wings." Dr Mourra would no doubt have preferred the run of a hospital in Marrakesh, instead of spreading his pretty, ineffectual peacock feathers in the royal gardens. The hazards of his position inspired real sympathy in all the courtiers. How can you resent a man who might be led to the gallows at any moment? Moreover, he was a most obliging fellow, who treated everyone regardless of their rank, tending to the neediest at a moment's notice. Countless times I saw him rush off to attend to a sick person in the Touarga neighbourhood, the area north of the ramparts where former slaves of the palace lived. Sidi would not have condoned such kindness.

So there you have it: I've started to tell you about the bag of snakes in which I spent most of my life. Just as proximity to power spawns monsters, so it can breed remarkable beings who, in days gone by, one might have called saints. As apart from Saher, and the inimitable Dr Mourra, Sidi's retinue teemed with faithless creatures of dubious integrity and morality. Over the course of my years with Sidi, I witnessed many startling incidents, alarming for a man of my culture, even one recycled into the role of court entertainer. However, in order to survive, I had to become an opportunist. I shed any qualms I had and learned to thrive on my colleagues' blunders. And there was considerable scope for action as they competed to spout nonsense. Their antics propelled me forward, and I took off like a bee to gather pollen for my stories, to sustain my sting. Sidi let others spew their drivel without batting an eyelid, but he wouldn't tolerate the slightest mistake from me. Having claimed the rank of "Fqih" on my first day, he never allowed me to fall into any form of mediocrity. Every single one of my comments had to be worth its weight in elegance and intelligence. Luckily, my comrades were of considerable help in nurturing and refining my work. Their baleful ignorance threw me lifelines, provided me with sticks to beat them, spools of thread from which I could weave fabulous stories. Sometimes, I felt as if I were merely tearing their birdbrained thinking asunder, letting my wit run riot, turning mockery into an art form. I exaggerated to the point of absurdity, sailed as close as I could to maliciousness without ever succumbing to it. How often I held back from a killer punchline, from hurtful words, spiteful words even! How many times did I want to make a monkey out of that vicious dwarf who enjoyed the king's favours . . . that jealous lump of black waste whose malice and dishonesty made him the most obnoxious member of our party. The man was a pest who spat his poison everywhere. A bundle of thorns who terrified us even though we could have floored him with a puff of our breath. To be honest, and I'm ashamed to say this, even though I harboured a respectful hatred for him, sometimes I also found him funny. He was particularly hilarious when he dug his fangs into a defenceless, mortified victim, his hollow laughter ringing out. It's almost impossible to fight ridicule when the audience is against you. That bastard found it easy to split his prey from the herd, like a wolf on the hunt, before feeding it to the pack. Sidi would smilingly encourage his blatherings as if they were his own. Or as we might say around here: the monarch willingly ate garlic with the dwarf's stinking mouth. Even if he did pick on others the dwarf never dared attack me head-on, only obliquely, in riddles, like a coward. He knew the chink in my armour and took every opportunity to remind everyone of it: "The apple never falls far from the tree," he'd say. Or: "Treacherous blood doesn't lie." And a thousand other references to my mutineer of a son, rotting away in the darkest prisons of the South. I wasn't going to stoop to his level by replying to the slander, though I didn't let it pass either. I polished my blade, waited to strike when he was least expecting it. Retaliation had to be proportionate to his provocations. He took the hits without reacting. When it came to contempt we were evenly matched. We settled into a truce, a precarious one, but as is so often the case in a cold war, it lasted longer than expected.

4

IF I HAD TO define my character in a single word, I'd suggest "connoisseur" as a suitable candidate. In matters of taste, whether clothes, music, poetry, scent or cuisine, my watchword was, without doubt, sophistication. I aspired to the finest in nature and human creativity. Although of humble origin, born in a tiny house in the shadows of the medina, my visits to the pasha's palace, where my father worked, had a profound influence on me from an early age. Moving between these two worlds, and given the choice, I picked my side pretty quickly. I plumped for the winners, and sought to acquire as much aristocratic refinement as I could. It's not surprising that my penchant for fine dining, aesthetics, social graces and lightness of touch became a matter of course in adulthood.

Starkly lit by neon strips, filled with noise and commotion, the staff dining room was the most inhospitable place in the royal palace. I only ate there when I had no choice, generally when the king was away on business. Otherwise, I preferred to wait in the antechamber for Sidi to finish eating before throwing myself on the leftovers from his copious meals. In truth, the king ate very little of the food Moha wheeled in on his trolley. As the valet went by, I'd always lean forward to inhale the escaping aroma from the solid silver domes that kept the food warm. In the morning we were entitled to a runny omelette with dried camel meat, and "*thousand-hole*" pancakes with eucalyptus honey, a range of clear soups and soft pastries. The blends of juices were continually reinvented: ginger, almond, guava, mango and heaps of seasonal fruit. The thought of the delectable, free feasts waiting for me at the palace was enough to get me up in the morning. I'd leap out of bed like a young lad, perform my ablutions and morning prayer, and be at the door to Sidi's apartments in a flash, ready for a day of laughter and cheer. Quite a few of us would cram into the royal antechamber early each morning, all for our own specific reasons, though I seemed to be the most ravenous. Ministers, generals and distinguished public servants clamoured for an audience, each armed with bulging folders and papers that required the boss's "immediate signature". But for that to happen, they needed the crucial go-ahead from Moha, the valet in charge of Sidi's meals. Stringy, angular, of noble appearance, and with uncannily roaming eyes, this slave's son had more power than all the top brass in the room. Having served the monarch for years, he'd been granted the privilege of gauging the king's mood before anyone else. His assessment was utterly invaluable, and he could decide to share it or keep it to himself. As he left Sidi's apartments, anxiously observed by all the high-ranking officials, Moha would either smile and nod (this meant the king could be disturbed without risk to life and limb, or, at best, the loss of your job), or he would lift his index finger and bend it like a scorpion's tail. That meant you were better off packing up your paperwork and postponing your visit until the next day. Top civil servants competed to smother the valet with friendliness as his clout made them all the more aware of their unimportance. Moha never fell for it, even though they were willing to grant him any special favours he desired in exchange for help. All he had to do was give them a little sign.

In the souk, the bazaar merchants gloomily call their stalls "tombs for life". And with good reason: they remain cooped up in them from dawn till dusk. I could say the same of the royal antechamber where I spent long periods of my life. While it had once been a place overflowing with laughter and insouciance, it later became bleak and distressing – as if the magic of old had never worked there, as if ghosts had sucked the quips, and all the fabulous singing and repartee, out of the air.

I learned to wait glumly until Sidi felt the need to summon me. I prayed for the moment I could rush to his bedside to devise my funny stories (throwing in a touch of lewdness, as he enjoyed the dirty bits). My head brimmed with such tales. Over the course of all those long years, when we were meant to be distracting the king and keeping him company, I never realised that the reverse would also be true: that I would one day miss Sidi's presence. The absence of his voice, his gaze, his orders, his sarcasm, his mannerisms, and even his rages, created an all-consuming void within me, and I had no way of filling it. I didn't know what to do with myself. My now-pointless humour turned black and heavy; my smile contorted into a dishonest grin. We had no choice but to wait, turning prayer beads in our hands in the hope of some miracle. Dr Mourra had been adamant: Sidi would no longer be of this world by the following Friday. He would not lead prayers at the mosque. Who wanted to believe him, though? I certainly didn't: nothing had yet happened to suggest such an abrupt decline. We often felt the monarch exaggerated his ailments. He enjoyed scaring us and we thought he'd be back on his feet in next to no time. How could we imagine we were on the brink of a violent and irreversible downfall? Only the week before, he had appeared in our antechamber without warning, and surprised me on the sofa where I like to sit. "Whatever you do, don't move," he said when I jumped to attention. Wearing a crocheted prayer cap and dressed in an off-white linen *gandoura*, he sat down next to me and propped his feet up on the ottoman. He seemed to be in a playful mood. One eyebrow raised, his lips breaking into a smirk, he said: "Remind me again of that passage in the *Thousand and One Nights* . . . that bit when Massoud climbs down from his tree and takes the unfaithful sultana right there and then on the ground." My word factory kicked into action before Sidi could even finish his sentence. Firing up my memory, I pulled open the drawers stuffed with stories and tales and, like a joyous child retrieving a confiscated toy, I threw myself headlong into the marvellous tale he had requested, not sparing a detail of the ten male slaves dressed as women and the orgiastic frolicking that took place around the fountain . . . Then, putting on my intellectual hat, I raised the tone a little, praising Scheherazade's subtlety of mind and her machinations. She defied death not only to save her skin, but also to keep the story going. It seemed as if it had only been a short while since Sidi hung on my every word, as Shahryar once listened with bated breath to his ravishing storyteller.

I watched Moha, the valet, try to get into the king's room with his trolley. He was unceremoniously dismissed, but he wouldn't give up. He kept at it and was again met with a barrage of insults. Sidi was refusing to feed himself. He avoided our company, burned incense despite his doctor's express prohibition and moaned until he was cross at himself for moaning, seething at his inability to hold back his tears. It pained me to hear him. Moha, too, and he cursed his helplessness as he stood there, arms dangling, stiff as a board, the king's door blocked by guards who stared straight through him as though he had suddenly become invisible, as though he no longer served any purpose now that Sidi had stopped eating. The days of the valet's power and arrogance were over. Both of our worlds were on the brink of collapse and neither of us knew what to do or even if there was anything to do. I couldn't understand how the other courtiers could carry on playing cards, bickering and squabbling, oblivious to their master's agony next door, ignoring death lurking near us. Moha prevented me from berating them. He said they were right: their cheerfulness could entice Sidi out of his seclusion. And, huddled on the floor by the sofa, his face drawn, having abandoned all pride in his role as saviour, Dr Mourra agreed. He beckoned to me to sit down and remain calm. Eyes half-closed, Saher stroked the strings of his oud, plucking an *arpeggio* of sombre chords which spiralled into the room like sighs. I guessed it was his way of crying. An almost human expression had appeared, as if by miracle, on Boudda's hideous face. It was hard to know what the dwarf was mourning, though: the loss of a great man or the loss of his own privileges. Wearing a red silk turban, and crouched next to the steps up to the *minbar*, the pulpit in the room, the fortune-teller Bilal, shuffled and reshuffled his cards, again and again, but they stubbornly delivered the same message. He grimaced as the black queen appeared, followed by an upside-down jack. Keen not to be found wanting, Moussa the herbalist had spent the night fashioning a potent charm to ward off bad luck, which somehow had to be slipped under the king's pillow. He paced up and down the room, stinking us out with his incense, swinging the burner back and forth, reciting incomprehensible prayers. The smoke from the alum stone and the *benzoin* resin – a combination said to protect against the evil eye – made me queasy. When Moussa handed the valet an unsavoury concoction for the patient to drink, Dr Mourra snapped out of his sorrow and objected to this point blank. Taking up his role as medic once more, he said: "There's no room for charlatans and quacks in this royal court. Pour that poison down the drain immediately." We were all dumbstruck: it was the first time we'd seen the doctor angry. Even though he'd just been branded a quack, Moussa was the first to burst out laughing, triggering general hilarity all round. Moha, whose aloofness was known to all, couldn't repress a smile either. I cast my eye over this odd scene – played out by old men I'd known for ages, but who often felt like strangers caught up in their own little worlds – and realised it was time to act.

Without wishing to boast, for years I was the only one who could defuse the king's anger. My fellow courtiers would all agree. I had perfected the art of improvisation and I could smooth over or turn around awkward situations with gentle mockery, or even dodge them entirely. It required trickery, bluster, flashes of wit and shock, anything to guide my blows. If I exaggerated the seriousness of a concern, it was only to subvert it later with a joke, and so on and so forth. I reminded anyone who wanted to listen that everything apart from death could be put right. I said that often, with hindsight, when tempers cooled, the cause of anger can seem utterly ludicrous. So this was how I turned things around, with sleights of hand, steering Sidi's foul moods towards friendly chatter. Although, I must admit, all this only worked if I first knew the ins and outs of the issue at stake.

There were times, however, when the monarch fell into a depression for no apparent reason. His crankiness led to a fierce and profound distrust of others. You couldn't get near him without being bitten. Yet I remember one May morning when I earned my stripes with the court hierarchy although still only a novice. And what a way to do it! The antechamber was packed with big shots from both the army and civil society, as well as a handful of foreign businessmen, immediately identifiable by their rosy cheeks and unfailing obsequiousness. We'd been hanging around for hours when Moha emerged from the king's chambers, looking rather forlorn. He pointed his bent index finger at the ceiling to warn us that a game of Russian roulette would involve less risk than a conversation with the king. He wasn't joking. I'm talking of a time, at the height of his glory, when the mere mention of Sidi's name would have people across the land quaking in their boots. He was only spoken about in hushed tones, with a glance over your shoulder, for fear of eavesdroppers who could turn you in . . . An ingrained paranoia permeated the whole city. The king's official photograph didn't help: his portrait was omnipresent, on shop walls, in homes, in government buildings and agencies, on the streets, in every single corner of the kingdom. It created a climate of fear. People felt His Majesty could spring out of the photograph at any moment and dole out punishment. His henchmen were not known for their kid gloves either. Countless men and women who had "compromised the country's security" disappeared. All the same, in that very paradoxical way of ours, and despite the terror he inspired, Sidi continued to be loved by his people. Within the palace and outside it.

One of his aunts, Lalla Yacout, had died and the king needed to be told as quickly as possible so the established protocol could be set in motion. Sidi had been especially close to his aunt and considered her his second mother. He would regularly enquire about her increasingly frail health, and he regretted, though accepted, her stubborn wish to live in a city of the North, far from the hustle and bustle of the capital. When he was a young boy, already rebellious and prone to tomfoolery, Lalla Yacout had protected the future king through many challenging times. The prince's pranks exasperated his father, a real stickler for rules, and this led to punishments of all kinds. Never on his aunt's watch though:

she'd snatch the boy from the clutches of the fire slaves, and throw herself at the king's feet, swearing by Allah that not a single hair on her nephew's head could be touched unless she was whipped first. His late Majesty would give in and the rascal would be let off the hook. It's fair to say that Sidi had harboured a real affection for this lady since those early days.

So one of us had to act as death's emissary and give him the news. I had firmly decided not to be that person. I shook my head when they all turned to me. It was a categorical no.

"Why am I the one who always has to do all the dirty work?" I protested.

"Because you're the best at it," the herbalist said.

The ministers, generals and courtiers present immediately agreed. But nothing would make me change my mind. I pulled down the hood of my djellaba and flicked my prayer beads out of my pocket.

"Ask the dwarf to do it," I said. "He's Sidi's favourite."

"All he does is bark," Bilal said.

"Well, we're not asking him to sing this bit of bad news. He just has to spit it out."

"Then we'll all get it in the neck," the herbalist said.

"Ask the doctor then – he knows all about corpses."

No-one laughed. Things were serious – we had to find a way. Sensing the mood was souring, the musician surprised us all by volunteering for the task.

"I'll deal with it," Saher said in a calm voice. "Death is part of life, isn't it?"

Moha frowned. The others glanced around warily, weighing up the potential risks of this development.

"No way, out of the question," I shouted. "You'll be squashed like a fly."

"Then you're the only one who can save him," the dwarf pointed out.

"I'm not worried," Saher said, getting to his feet.

I loved this man too much to sacrifice him to the flames without a fight. They were right: no-one else but me could deal with the matter without risking some major fallout. Putting on a brave front, I got up and took several small steps towards the line of fire. The henchmen parted to let me through. I knocked gently on the door only to hear what sounded like an angry beast's roar ricochet off the ceiling. I pushed the door further and, with some difficulty, slipped my head through the folds of the garnet-coloured, velvet curtains.

"Get out of here!" the king yelled.

Sprawled across a bed, shored up by a mountain of cushions, a compress across his forehead, Sidi looked like he was having one of his bad days.

"If Your Majesty would just allow me a second . . ."

"No, I won't allow you."

"To just say . . ."

"Get out," he snarled.

"Your Majesty, I'm the biggest fool of all time."

"Will you get out of my sight, you jackass! I'm not in the mood . . ."

"Ah, Your Majesty, funny you should say that."

"Guards!" he screamed.

Two henchmen appeared.

"Before giving me the hundred lashes that I rightly deserve, please let me point out that had I, the jackass that I am, married your aged aunt yesterday I would now be a millionaire."

"What's my aunt got to do with any of this?"

"May she rest in peace, Your Majesty. Lalla Yacout passed away last night, shortly before morning prayer."

The king jumped out of bed, got dressed as quickly as he could and stepped into action.

These were the sort of situations that, at the height of my glory, I used to be able to manage in a flash. But now things were more complicated. People don't improve with age – they're merely altered by it. If you're lucky, your better traits might be preserved, but the less flattering aspects of your personality will inevitably worsen. I know what I'm talking about, having closely observed my old master's character over time.

Now, once again, I had to act with speed: the king's health was deteriorating fast. I couldn't just sit back and twiddle my thumbs. Despite mulling it over endlessly, I couldn't see how to lighten the mood. Yet there was one solution that I continued to discount as it offended me – and that was to resort to the services of the young princess Sofia. Such a move felt more like a surrender to me, but I could no longer afford to pander to my ego. The little brat was the only one who could get us out of the mess and we all knew it. I reluctantly told Moha, whose eyes always jiggled the moment an idea pleased him. He slipped out of the room and headed to the princes' gallery in the south wing of the palace, reappearing half an hour later with the tiny know-it-all by his side. The princess walked through the antechamber, briefly stopped to chat with Dr Mourra (not deigning to acknowledge our little bows) and nonchalantly continued on her way. Lilliputian, dressed in an elegant white dress embroidered at the hems, her impudent face crowned by blonde hair plaited into the form of a tiara, she cast a withering eye over the courtiers, to make sure that we knew we were amateurs, incapable of the very task for which we were so handsomely paid. No matter how much I cursed her, I had to admit she really was a cherub sent by the Heavens. She stood skipping, mischievous and impish, before Sidi's apartments. Having been ordered to allow her in whenever she wanted, the minders swung the door wide open. She let out a kind of bird call, then another, even louder, which Sidi immediately and playfully echoed. I heard her run to the four-poster bed and snuggle up against her grandfather's diseased body. Although usually of rather dour disposition, Moha the valet put his arms around me and hugged me tight. He praised the brilliance of my idea, kicked himself for not having thought of it. Sidi had finally come back to life and that's what mattered. The antechamber became more animated. Everyone dusted themselves down; the card players got back to their bickering, the herbalist's incense burner swung into action and Saher's music sped up. Seeing the dwarf dance a frenzied jig, Dr Mourra recovered his good humour and usual composure. Our relief was complete when we saw the king head out to the gardens, holding his granddaughter's hand. "Long live the king!" the slaves sang, and I managed to insult them by joining in.

5

SIGNING UP TO PALACE life is like joining a sect: membership is all-embracing, irrevocable. Once you're a devotee, there's no turning back. Or if there is, you leave either on your knees, or feet first. It's a pact with darkness. Everything beyond the boundaries of the holy institution has to be discarded. No blunder is tolerated, only unwavering, unquestioning obedience. You become part of the decor, on a par with the fixtures and fittings, the trees in the garden, the hordes of slaves. Nonetheless, I had, and I still have, a life outside the palace, however illusory, however flawed.

I never saw my wife age or my children grow up. Yet I'm no more a bad husband than I am an unworthy father: I just kept my head down in a place where I had limited choices, a world beyond my control. When you board the golden palace train, you're allowed only brief and very occasional stopovers. Images scroll past: you're nothing more than a remote spectator on an increasingly alien world, without a grip on its reality. Despite appearances, I didn't give up. No matter how much I fell for the lavish comfort of court life, and found myself sliding down its starlit slope, I never stopped coldly assessing myself. Even if the sole purpose of my existence was to please my master, the love I bore my family remained unbroken: a real and tender love, despite its many wounds. For all my years of happy confinement in the palace, I was careful never to sever the tenuous thread that bound me to my tribe. It wasn't easy. I fought, schemed as much as I could, walked all sorts of fine lines, and trusted that the quality of the moments I devoted to them would compensate for their brevity. Yet we all know that only a part of an artist's life is his own. My time was the exclusive property of His Majesty. On a good day, Sidi would toss me crumbs of it, as if to a beggar, and I kept them warm in my unsteady hands, turning them into rare opportunities that I meekly offered my family. The glittery court had taught me the value of time, its transience, its preciousness. In the medina, people are unaware of how they squander it . . . The way others lounge around all day in cafés, and watch passers-by, is beyond the comprehension of my palace friends. Yet it didn't shock me in the old days to drift around in the main square, the Jemaa el-Fnaa, with Ben Brahim by my side. While I devoted myself to his miraculous flights of poetry, he dreamed in quatrains of the chiselled bodies and virile features that set his blood on fire . . . sometimes they even got me flustered, too.

One day, in the antechamber, in Sidi's presence, Saher paused between two songs and said:

"Depending on whether one is rich or poor, time does not flow in the same way."

I was particularly fond of this man, but I did not always agree with him.

"Time is the same for everyone, what are you saying? It's pure mathematics."

"Yes and no," Saher said with a smile.

"In my humble opinion," I said, "the passing of time is one of the most democratic features of this world . . . the fairest. Rich and poor age the same."

Saher enjoyed my company. He was not seeking to contradict me in any way or upset me.

The herbalist saved us by turning to the musician.

"Please explain what you mean."

Saher reached for his instrument and strummed a few chords to help him think.

"The hours of the affluent man are a constant race. They're filled with urgency and stress. Time whizzes by like a comet in the night. Pressure is constant."

He started to tune his instrument, placing its rounded belly against his ear — as if to make us assess and grasp the validity of this idea.

"And what about the poor man's hours?" Bilal asked as he shuffled his cards.

"Oh! I lived those in another life. They're generally swallowed up by oblivion, mired in deadly lethargy, lost in the apathy of weariness. They're the hardest to get through . . ."

We thought his comments made good sense. The dwarf Boudda, his ears twitching as ever, said:

"That must be the reason why the poor fear death less than we do."

"I don't understand," the herbalist said.

"Because they've nothing to lose!" he replied with a

malicious hiss, adding: "According to our learned musician, the poor man's time is worthless. When the destitute bite the dust, they're essentially heading home, back to what they've always known, if you like."

"What do you mean?" the herbalist protested.

"It's simple for them – there's no point making a meal out of passing from one form of obscurity to another. It's a mere formality."

If the king hadn't smiled at that point, I'm not sure any of us would have approved of this crass comment. Yet Sidi felt it was the worthiest observation of the whole evening – and we agreed, unanimously, that it was indeed witty and insightful.

To find time for yourself was a real challenge.

Knowing how to take advantage of the talents you'd been born with was another. In my early days at court, my aim was to achieve the recognition I felt I deserved. With age it stopped being a priority. This didn't prevent my skills from leading me astray, however. My appointment to the pompous and highly coveted role of "attendant to the royal sleep" was no gift – far from a sinecure. My ability to tell stories better than my fellow courtiers caused me no end of trouble and stoked up unimaginable jealousy. To know that I was alone with the king infuriated my peers. I was credited with the most unlikely conspiracies, accused of countless evils: the sacking of a random person I had never met, the dismissal of an official who was a total stranger to me, the unfortunate death of a general in a car accident, the ousting of a governor on the fringes of the Sahara . . . I was blamed each time. In one way or another, my shadow hovered over all the king's brutal decisions. And there were many. I was credited with fuelling the king's anger, which was utterly unfair. Try as I might to avoid clashes, to bring people together, conflict always caught up with me and made my life miserable. I had to take on my foes. I got sucked into a warlike mentality, and it forced me to carry out the occasional pre-emptive strike – to use my master's terminology.

My closeness to His Majesty filled me with a pride I found hard to conceal. It gave me power, and I realised the extent of it from my rivals' green-eyed scowls. The truth is I did control the most dangerous weapon in our absolute monarchy: the king's ear. I could flatter or demolish someone just by tacking a little hint on the end of an ordinary sentence. A simple comment, *en passant*, was all that was needed to cast a doubt in Sidi's mind. And in our world, where there is no time to waste, why burden yourself with any compunction about checking facts? You make a snap decision. Plain and simple. So what if a life, or a career, is lost in a split second? When you have the king's ear, you are as mighty as the king. Our relationship made me the man I am today, and God alone knows how I struggled not to abuse my role.

When the king withdrew for the night, I'd wait for a sign from the chamberlain, Monsieur Brek, before slipping into his bedroom. Sidi didn't like too much light. He lived in permanent twilight, a gloom in which it was hard to make anything out. Although I knew the exact positions of the armchairs, stands, lamps and the low table, as well as all the other bits of furniture, I inevitably tripped up each time.

Sometimes I'd exaggerate a fall, and end up face down on the plush wool carpet, to amuse the king – a little warm-up act before I settled on the ottoman at the end of the bed to undertake the urgent task of preparing my master for sleep. The moment he put his book down, I'd spring into action with a joke and then produce the stories Sidi expected of me. Preferably, these would be stories I had never told before, which was no mean feat. Even by giving free rein to my imagination, and tapping into my boundless stock of readings, I found it difficult to replenish my tales all the time. I'd parody a standard plot, warm up old scenes, rehash bits and then add my latest frills. I'd proceed with such care, with such subtlety, that I eventually fell for the story myself. I'd lay it on thick. Every word, expression and intonation served to underpin the narrative, which I embroidered with a thousand and one follies. I only lowered my voice at the sound of Sidi's first snores. A happy purring, which I welcomed every time, proof that my master's dreams had gently taken over from my stories. Sometimes, however, Sidi would drop off without a noise, not even the hint of a whimper, nothing, and this put me in a difficult position as I didn't know when to draw the curtains or when to tuck my own restless characters up in bed. I had a few tricks: I'd thread the odd unexpected word into my story, the kind of expression that would make a corpse jump out of its coffin. For instance, I'd get the caliph Harun ar-Rashid to hitch a ride in a lift at the time of the Abbasid dynasty. If the king didn't react, I'd stand up quietly, put on my babouches and creep out of the room. But these subterfuges were not without risk, and now and again they backfired. The day I placed the eighth-century poet Abu Nuwas in a helicopter to meet his lover in the desert, Sidi was so wracked by laughter that he didn't sleep all night. If these spasms of irrepressible mirth struck just as I was winding down, I had to change tack quickly and find ways to coax Sidi to sleep. Bedtime stories were fraught with peril. Either things worked out, and I could calmly head home, or I paid for it dearly till morning came.

Like most of the courtiers, I owned a cosy house in an upmarket neighbourhood of the capital, ten minutes from the palace – all thanks to His Majesty's largesse. I don't want to shock you, but I have to point out that this home was given to me with furnishings of the highest quality, a garage containing a valuable German saloon car, and even a bedroom, which, a week after I moved in, was occupied by a surprisingly ravishing wife "provided" by the royal chambers. Mina came from the Touarga neighbourhood and she gave me three beautiful children. It didn't take long for this brunette with hazelnut eyes, and a love of good food and poetry, to seduce me. You see, admittance to the palace led to an all-inclusive offer that was hard to turn down. Such courtesies were dictated by security concerns, because, of course, we had daily access to the king's private quarters. Mina was not an informer, strictly speaking, but she had once been employed as a secretary in the palace. So the courtiers could not really object to the wives offered them. I have no memory of my comrades protesting at all. Indeed, some who were already married didn't hesitate to tie the knot a second time with the young thing the royal office "imposed" on them.

The king's word was law – and his cheerful decree made many happy. Truth be told, I came out of this matter of marriage rather well. I belong to a generation used to arranged marriages. They were the norm. Despite what people say, they work better than today's kind. What's more, after the wonderful invention of photography, many no longer had any nasty surprises on their wedding night. Unlike our parents, we knew exactly what we were getting. In the old days, couples met, got to know each other, lived and loved, raised families, aged and died together. I'm telling you what I think, however archaic and reactionary it sounds to my children. The fact is, today's marriages have lost the fire and magic of bygone days.

Organising the marriages of a bunch of fellows like us was a considerable achievement for the royal secretariat. Boudda's case, however, caused them a serious headache. Despite extensive searches, no lady dwarf was found in the Touarga neighbourhood. The woman assigned to him was taller by at least a whole torso, plus a head crowned with frizzy hair. Though he happily agreed to marry this giantess, she wasn't that delighted with her lot. His unflattering physique aside, the dwarf's despicable character and notorious malice made him doubly repugnant.

Moussa, the herbalist, was the least fortunate amongst us. Though he was granted the privilege of marrying into royal blood, a cousin several times removed of Sidi's, the young lady weighed a good hundred kilos, if not more. Far from ugly, her regular features gave her a rather friendly face. And because she was of a happy and brassy disposition people quickly forgot her vastness. Intimate relations, however, were off limits for old Moussa: his fleshy princess wasn't interested in any form of sex. Her rolls of fat were a real turn-off anyway, a blatant assault on the senses.

The one who got off lightly was, without doubt, Bilal the fortune-teller. Having been forewarned in a vision about the wife he was going to be offered, he decided to cut his losses and announce to all and sundry that he preferred men. He braved insults, sleazy remarks, degrading names, the lot. He stood firm. Whenever they had a go at him, he took refuge in his cards – like Saher in his music. He simply withdrew from the world. Boudda did his utmost to fire his poisoned barbs at him, but he couldn't harm him. That's how Bilal escaped the woman he'd spotted in his future. Given the attacks he endured, she can't have been a beauty. As generous as ever, Sidi found another way to reward Bilal and allocated him a driver who looked like a Greek god.

Saher was the odd one out in our group. Seeing all these marriages taking place, one after another, he feared he would have to accept a similar fate despite being madly in love with his next-door neighbour from his childhood years: a tall, attractive girl with black eyes called Zohra. One blissful evening, after he had played a wonderful love song by the great Mohamed Abdel Wahab – a desperately sad story that moved the king to tears – he decided to try his luck:

"You see, Your Majesty, I too love a woman, and my devotion to her is just like the poet's in that song."

"Who is this woman for whom an artist such as you is willing to give his life?" the king asked.

"She's called Zohra, Your Majesty. We got engaged when she was a teenager. She's still waiting for me."

As the king thought about this, Saher added:

"May I humbly request your blessing, Your Majesty? I would very much like to make her my wife."

Boudda the dwarf butted in:

"Is this not an insult to the Touarga ladies? The most beautiful women from deepest Africa who live right here on our doorstep. Might our musician be a little bit racist?"

Seeing my friend stutter, I intervened, against my better judgment.

"Saher has nothing against people of a different origin from him. We are proud of our country's diversity. Saher, a racist? That's absurd. The proof is he's fond of you, Boudda, despite your being a midget."

Seeing the situation was about to turn nasty, the king decided to give the musician's marriage his blessing and he shut the vicious troublemaker down. Moreover, with a swipe of the hand, he indicated to the chamberlain that he would cover the costs of the event.

What about the doctor, you might ask? As he'd already lived in the palace with his wife and children for years, he was never offered anything. I think he rather regretted it.

6

THE ULTIMATE PUNISHMENT FOR a courtier is to be stripped of his dignity, to lose that which a human being holds most dear, even if dignity had not been foremost on his mind when he first walked into the palace. In theory, you're meant to leave your ego, self-esteem and other forms of pride at the palace door before you enter, like a pair of old babouches that might dirty the alabaster floors. Yet despite our best intentions, so many of us find it hard to give up our self-respect.

Disgrace! A word that only those who have eaten from a tyrant's outstretched hand can fully comprehend. Not one of us in Sidi's inner circle managed to escape the agony of its poison. I now see that it is kinder to sack a close associate outright than to leave him dangling, in limbo, for an unspecified period, whether it be an evening, a week, a month, a year, a whole life even, as that sentences him to doubt. And doubt is the worst form of retribution: it gnaws at the heart and guts, keeps you awake at night; it's a rotten tooth that is neither treated nor removed. The torment drives you mad. This is how it is for any wretch who falls into disgrace at court: he's neither fully in, nor fully out. He's subjected to an insidious form of persecution, first by the monarch, the mastermind behind it all, then by his peers, his supposed friends and accomplices – despicable individuals who, nails dug into the armrests of their comfortable chairs, fight to expel the victim from the golden inner circle with a deluge of insults, happy that they've not been picked on themselves. Spare a thought for the man who stumbles, for there is no pity in the king's palace. He will experience an unimaginable hollowness, a loneliness, a complete loss of all bearings. His life means nothing, neither to himself, nor to others. He has tripped into a void and his fall is endless: down and down he goes, disoriented, searching for a hand to catch him. Crushed by scorn, and the haughtiness of those who have forgotten him, the victim's wait drags on and on. It turns time itself into an enemy. But how to fight back? With what weapons? You've only got blanks and sputtering squibs. Resentment is just as pointless: dejection simply leads to sterile brooding. How do you resist a dirty look anyway, a barbed comment, whispers that are hushed the moment you walk into a room? How do you deal with pity, even if it's sincere, a single sympathetic tap on the shoulder when you're on your knees?

Disgrace! What an odious word. I understand what it means now. I've seen how far it reaches, endured the indifference and isolation of its depths. It is a place of banishment, without solace, without tears or whimpering where you simply float in the vacuum of your destitution, not knowing when, or how, or indeed if salvation's light might finally break through. You survive, head bowed, wishing the hours away, silence swallowed by more silence. Your restless nights no longer bother to solicit sleep. Instead sleep looks down at you, its glassy eyes filled with your own tormented reflection. You're stuck, resigned, defenceless, undermined, vanquished, alone. Unbearably alone. Later, I'll tell you how I plummeted into this dreaded purgatory. The mere mention of it bewilders me still, twenty-five years later.

One day, a highly eminent minister, whose name I will not reveal out of kindness, fell prey to one of Sidi's blind rages. The news spread through the palace corridors: everyone from lowly servant to army general, humble foreman to chamberlain, Touarga slave to veteran courtier, tittered at the man's shocking misfortune. The minister concerned – and I know what I'm talking about as I witnessed the whole matter first-hand – had incurred the king's wrath on a day when he was in a particularly foul mood. The idiot hadn't checked with any of us before submitting his half-baked documents to His Majesty. If he'd bothered to pay attention to Moha's bent forefinger, clearly visible from the door into the drawing room, like a scorpion poised to sting the first person who dared approach, he might have saved his fat backside. Instead, in the way that many long-serving politicians end up assuming that their virtue and wisdom will protect them from trouble, our minister believed he was untouchable – in fact, he was convinced that talent was the only fuel necessary for the smooth running of the kingdom. A grievous mistake in a country where the monarch wields absolute power. The common good is of little consequence when the king is feeling grouchy: a bout of insomnia one night can grind the whole nation to a halt for months, without anyone being able to object. As the old adage goes here: no-one is irreplaceable in the king's court. Indeed, the moment a reckless freethinker starts to dream of grandeur, to delude himself that he's a lynchpin, he gets sucked into a mire he'd never previously been aware of, pulled down by the tentacles of an invisible octopus. Sticking your head above the parapet is not without risk in the king's inner circle. The sort of suppleness of neck observed in tortoises can prove more beneficial. And one beautiful spring day, our friend the minister was to bear the brunt of the king's fury.

We were having lunch when the shameless halfwit strode into the great hall with such purpose that we were convinced he was about to announce that an earthquake had struck the North of the country, or that a tsunami had swept the outskirts of the capital away, or perhaps even that we were on the brink of war with our eastern neighbour. Everyone waited in silence as he approached Sidi, his demeanour sombre. He leaned over the king's shoulder, whispered into his ear and placed a blue folder on the small table near the telephone. His gall, the boldness of his attitude, could only mean that this was an emergency, that there wasn't a minute to spare: decisions had to be made forthwith. We stared at Sidi, expecting him to jump up, summon his ministers and race to his office to direct operations. Yet, instead, he appeared to be thinking, gazing blankly at the ceiling. I knew that look, that expressionless face, when Sidi's eyes froze, and no word emerged from his mouth, as if the world had stopped turning. The courtiers held their breath: a moment of stillness before a desert storm. Turning to the guards, the king said in a voice that would have been gentle had bile not oozed from it: "Remove this animal from my sight. I don't want to see him anymore."

There was an established code of conduct between the king and his security retinue. From the tone of his voice and the sternness of his stare, the officers had a choice: either they grabbed the poor man by the hood of his djellaba, dragged him, cowering, through the palace corridors and across the gardens to the front gates and hurled him onto the tarmac, the ultimate humiliation; or they escorted him in a more or less civilised manner, though equally upsettingly, towards the exit, sandwiching him between their massive bodies. Knowing how things went in the palace, the minister decided on a different course of action . . .

So began this most unusual affair, the likes of which no-one in the palace, in living memory, had ever encountered before. Running ahead of the bodyguards who were coming for him, themselves a little hesitant and embarrassed – as this was a high-ranking official, and one of Sidi's closest allies, after all – the minister left the room and headed to the royal stables, with a horde of guards in tow. The head groom certainly didn't understand what the kerfuffle was about. Thinking the king was about to carry out an impromptu visit, he swung the doors open and whistled to round up his staff. The minister burst in, went straight into an empty stall that was about to be mucked out, and sat on the ground with his back against a bale of straw. The guards watched in bewilderment as his white djellaba became stained with manure.

"Sidi has deemed me to be an animal," the minister said to the head groom. "So be it: my place is now amongst these animals. I will live, eat and sleep with other beasts. I will only leave this place, reduced as I am to the state of an animal, when ordered to do so by my master."

The assembled men looked at each other in desperation, unsure of how to deal with the strangeness of the situation. The minister had, quite clearly, lost his mind. Several big cheeses appeared to help sort out the situation, but they, too, could only note the "animal's" state of mental disarray. Nevertheless, they tried to reason with their friend, who didn't want to hear a word. In fact, he grew ever more frantic and unruly. He scraped the manure from the ground and smeared it over his head, repeating: "Animals live with animals, stink like animals, and that's the way it should be. Sidi said I was an animal, my place is amongst other animals, Sidi never gets creatures wrong, I should know as I've proudly served him for half my life . . ."

The guards made a weak attempt to remove him, but the grand mufti – who happened to be passing by – stopped them, suggesting they call Dr Mourra immediately. The doctor appeared with his black briefcase, his paunch and his good humour. He shooed the crowd of curious onlookers away. He asked the groom for a bottle of fresh water and went into the stall to talk to the patient. He greeted him, crouched down beside him and started to chat, as if they were just having one of their usual conversations. After a while, by some miracle, he managed to get the minister to swallow a sedative – one that was strong enough to knock out a horse, so to speak. He then slipped out of the stables, as if nothing remarkable had occurred.

One of the officials ended up seeking the king's advice. He found the matter hilarious. His courtiers, too, couldn't contain their laughter, and they yelled obscenities and jibes. The dwarf suggested a possible liaison between the minister and Sidi's prize stallion– and he reminded everyone of a recent news item: a young farmer had been found dead next to his horse, choked by the animal's semen, a discharge so sudden and abundant that the poor man's stomach and lungs had been flooded – the fellow had not been able to resist the beast's majestic organ. "That's the way it goes with love stories," Moussa added. "They rarely end well."

Bilal, his eyes on his fortune-telling cards, offered another interpretation. He recalled the day they'd watched a mare be presented to a stud. As the Arab stallion mounted the brown mare, the same minister had commented on the unique eroticism of the mating creatures. Bilal remembered how the minister's eyes glistened that day. The way he had spoken of the gloriously alluring coupling had produced a little frisson in him, too. In light of this, Bilal decided that the romance had more likely been between the minister and the brown mare – her muscular rump did, undeniably, exude a certain sensuality. Nothing in the cards contradicted this possibility either. The more Sidi laughed, the more the jokers laid it on. From time to time, they glanced at me, expecting me to add some scathing wisecrack of my own, to seal the minister's farcical fate for ever. I didn't react. I have never been able to laugh at a man when he is down.

Callous to the end, Sidi decreed that the minister should spend the night in the stables. He did concede, however, that the man be brought a platter of food and a blanket.

Forget dignity, this was how low some of my peers would stoop to keep their place in the sun. After all these years at Sidi's side, the depths of human ignominy and dishonour no longer surprise me.

7

WHAT COULD BE MORE natural for a fortune-teller than to attain personal glory through a dream? Bilal was guided (coerced and bullied, too, if truth be told) to the palace via a crooked path paved with visions. Nightmares, in fact, as Sidi pictured himself one night being rolled from the top of a rocky mountain straight into a valley of quicksand, clutching the heir to the throne in his arms. It was a ghastly, desperate scene. He held his weeping child as high as he could while he sank lower and lower into the sludge. The nightmare caused Sidi considerable distress. Every time he went to sleep, he felt as though his throne were teetering on the brink, swaying on a pair of stilts, close to collapse. He would wake with a start, his face awash with sweat, his heart thumping. The anguish brought on terrible insomnia and exacerbated his crotchetiness. The king's clique of courtiers contradicted and challenged each other in their various interpretations of the dream. Great sages, seasoned fortune-tellers, and well-known charlatans, visited the sovereign's antechamber, one after another. Some felt the dream heralded Sidi's grand plan to reclaim the deserts in the South, a gift of new territory to consolidate his young prince's future reign. Others construed the dream as proof that the king and the land of his illustrious forefathers formed but one coherent, unbreakable entity . . . Even more of this subservient gibberish was reeled off, but Sidi rejected it wholesale. None of it made sense to him.

When we ran out of options, and were on the point of giving up, we generally turned to the queen mother. She had a knack for solving intractable problems. As we had little chance of coming across her in the palace corridors, Moha volunteered to speak to her. We greatly admired the queen mother, and particularly loved seeing her on festival days, in her silk caftan, as she went to give the king her best wishes. I found it very touching to see Sidi bending over, almost on his knees, kissing his mother's palm and then the back of her hand. "Paradise is to be found under our mothers' feet," he would say. "Make sure you kiss them every morning, and with luck you'll enter its sacred gates."

Even though the queen mother was not my mother (and I do sincerely regret that), I once really did find paradise under her feet. I swear I did. It was a long time ago, on the eve of Eid-el-Kabir. I wasn't a big fan of this feast day, which I found rather time-consuming and gory – but mostly very expensive as my whole tribe would travel up from the South and camp in front of my door, expecting me, the "extremely rich companion to the king", to gift them some poor sheep to sacrifice. That year, I didn't have any money for the flock of sheep they were demanding. I worried myself sick all night, unable to solve the problem in my mind. Whole families were squatting in the shade of my garden walls, waiting for the livestock I had accustomed them to, as if it were their due. Shirking my duty would have cheated my tribe of their celebration, and lost me all credibility in their eyes. I was, after all, the only one of our humble lineage to have had the good fortune to defy gravity and reach society's upper echelons. I was cornered, and my pride prevented me from asking Sidi for a loan. I felt distressed, yet hopeful, too, confident that people like me, who had been born lucky, were generally saved in the nick of time. Indeed, the very next day, the queen mother herself rescued me. As I arrived at the palace, I saw her watering some garden beds filled with shimmering bright flowers, their shapes striking and sensual. Such a vision immediately triggered an irrepressible outpouring of Ben Brahim's verse, and from my mouth came a poem to the glory of *a rose watering a rose . . . the whisper of the breeze, pearls of dew*, and other such early-morning smarminess.

The queen smiled and said:

"You've caught me off guard, Mohamed. I have nothing to offer you in exchange for your words."

"A queen always has something to offer her faithful servant, Lalla."

"What do you want? My shawl?"

"One of your beautiful embroidered babouches, Lalla."

"Why only one?" she said, amused enough to remove both her slippers. "Take the pair."

"One alone is enough, Lalla. If I had two, my wife might be tempted to wear them. And, as we know, no-one must defile a shrine once visited by a heavenly being."

The queen smiled, still puzzled, while a servant immediately brought her another pair of shoes.

That evening, in the antechamber, I described the muddle I'd got myself in to with the courtiers. I explained everything from my pitiful financial situation to the swarms of bumpkins besieging my home. I asked for my colleagues' help as I was going to auction a slipper belonging to the queen mother in Sidi's presence. Everyone found the idea hilarious, and original. They agreed to go along with it, though no-one let Boudda the dwarf in on the secret as he was more than capable of betraying me and undermining the whole stunt. Shortly before dinner, I extracted the precious object from the hood of my djellaba, and placed it on the table. "Gentlemen," I said, as if I were some sort of street hawker, "I would never have sought to sell a treasure of this value had my tribe not been in such dire need on the day before the Eid celebrations. So it is with a heavy heart that I offer this cherished gift to the highest bidder, a present Lalla Oum Sidi herself gave me: a babouche stitched with gold thread and embossed with her illustrious initials."

My opening bid was met with lukewarm enthusiasm. I had set the price so high that the king, who had been vaguely following proceedings from across the room, went back to his book, as if smelling a rat. I reminded the courtiers of our master's motto, applying it to the circumstances: "If paradise can be found under our mothers' feet, it is even more likely to be under their babouches, is it not? And the gold embroidery on this slipper is a tiny foretaste of heaven." The king smiled, but didn't budge.

Boudda left the room the moment the auction got under way, just as Saher and Dr Mourra were doing their best to ramp up the bidding. An army general joined in and egged the visiting guests on. I found I had the eloquence of an auctioneer: I chided the stinginess of some, pandered to the generosity of others, ignited that craving for domination and ownership that rears its head when people try to outbid each other. The grand mufti was sitting alone on his prayer mat and suddenly threw himself into the ring with a crazily high bid: fifty thousand dirhams – a whole cascade of real, tinkling and shiny coins, a whopping amount. Everyone was stunned. Luckily a burst of laughter from Sidi broke our stupor, and, with a wry smile, he announced that he'd pay. We never understood what got into the grand mufti: he was usually so calm and measured. He had got entirely carried away, but his outburst at least prompted the king to increase the bid. Sidi retrieved his mother's slipper and turned to me: "I know your tricks, Mohamed! Don't think for a minute that you fooled me. This is a gift for your flea-bitten tribe – wish them a happy Eid from me." I bowed humbly, delighted that the image of a *rose watering a rose* had brought me such bounty – enough to turn yours truly into a livestock breeder, had I so wanted.

But let us get back to Bilal and how he came to be at the king's palace. At Moha's request, the queen received the courtiers and promptly directed them to a lady of her seraglio named Tamou. She was known to be a bit of a sorceress and a specialist in the secret language of the soul. By all accounts, this woman with creepy eyes dabbled in the occult and deployed it to decipher outlandish dreams. Yet the moment she heard that the king had had this vision, she wanted nothing to do with it. She told us to consult the fortune-teller who had been her master, a man named Bilal, who lived as a hermit in a remote cave overlooking a hamlet in the High Atlas mountains. This sufi sage reputedly knew how to elucidate portents and omens of all sorts. He was an undisputed master who had been raised to the rank of marabout by the people of the village. They had even built a *koubba* to house his mortal remains one day.

The queen mother took the matter very seriously and sent her guards to fetch this fortune-teller as quickly as possible. After days walking along craggy, winding mountain paths, the guards found the hamlet. A short distance above it they spotted a cave, in front of which a herbalist burned incense while mumbling prayers. This was Moussa, Bilal's faithful servant. He led the guards to his master, who was sitting reading his cards, surrounded by candles of varying lengths.

"I was waiting for you, gentlemen," he said.

"The queen asked us to . . ."

"My bundle of possessions is packed, as is the one belonging to my attendant. We're ready to follow you."

The guards exchanged worried glances.

The men later found themselves in the royal antechamber, waiting to be received by the king.

That day Bilal shuffled and reshuffled his cards while Moussa the herbalist smoked us out with his incense-burner – just as they would for the next thirty years. I still remember Bilal's first visit to the king's office as if it were yesterday. The meeting was meant to take a quarter-of-an-hour. It lasted the whole morning. Fortune-teller and monarch stayed cooped up like two old friends. Nothing of their conversation filtered out. We never knew what was said between them that morning, but Sidi seemed jauntier the following day, and Bilal remained with us from then on. The fortune-teller's only stipulation was that he wished to keep the herbalist with him. Sidi readily agreed.

8

MY FATHER USED TO say: "There's a rock in the sky waiting to fall on the head of the first man who dares to belittle himself in public." He didn't say this to raise a laugh, as some might, or to be overly virtuous. This orbiting boulder, my father said, had never dropped on anyone; it remained suspended in space, as it had since the beginning of time, spinning, searching for an unlikely victim. What I mean by this is that autobiography can only reveal fragments of the truth about ourselves: the most favourable parts. Otherwise, I'd already be dead, flattened by that dreaded, tireless rock.

How much more convoluted must this story get before I mention the wound that has refused to heal after all these years: how my eldest son had the brilliant idea of overturning my whole life's work in a single morning? This cursed son ended up in the darkest prison of the South, as far from his fellow men as possible, buried at the bottom of a pit, deep in the barren stretches of the desert, a place of death befitting his transgression, with only ghosts of his kind to haunt him. Yet I was made out to be his gravedigger in this tragedy. I became a monster, a nobody, a dirty sell-out. I was unfairly accused of everything; I was judged and condemned without trial. In any case, my story is not complete unless I reveal my son's role in it, unless I describe how my own flesh and blood nearly dragged me down with him in his fall. And how I returned home every evening to find my wife in a state of perpetual mourning, a mother severed from her love: her firstborn child. So long as Abel remained in a regular prison, it was all right: she didn't stop being courteous and considerate despite the friction between us. She never missed a single Thursday – visiting day at the prison – when she would take him a basket of provisions, mostly clean linen and dark-tobacco cigarettes. Even though she was miserable, Mina returned home serene in the evening, her heart at peace. She even joked that her son's imprisonment meant she saw him more often than before. Though, of course, it wasn't as she would have liked because she couldn't hold her boy in her arms, but still. She said it was a comfort to know that he was in good health, to be able to talk to him despite the din in the vast visiting room divided by walls of wire mesh: crowded families on one side and prisoners on the other, and behind them a guard walking back and forth non-stop, listening in. Then one day it stopped. Abel vanished, just like that, and no-one provided an explanation. If Mina hadn't had two teenagers waiting at home, she would undoubtedly have lost her mind. Still she carried on visiting the central prison. She turned up every Thursday at ten o'clock on the dot, with a basket of provisions, clean laundry and dark-tobacco cigarettes. On feast days she even added a box stuffed with cakes to brighten the delivery up. The prison guards would shoo her away, but she returned all the same. She would sit on the bench in front of the huge studded-iron gate and stay put all morning. What was she waiting for? I wouldn't be able to tell you – perhaps for a carrier pigeon to come and settle on her lap with news of her boy? Beggars swarmed around, knowing that, sooner or later, she would share out the provisions equally, linen and cigarettes. Almost a year went by before she gave up on these futile, painful visits. She could no longer bear to hear the prison guards tell her: "The king ordered the transfer of the mutineers to a military barracks . . ." "No, Madame, no-one knows where that is." That was the root of the nightmare for me: the words "the king ordered" implied his entourage – in other words, me and my companions. In Mina's mind, I was privy to the king's plans, and that tore my home life apart. One evening, just before going to sleep, Mina leaned over my shoulder and whispered: "So when are you going to give me my son back?" I lay there, stunned, powerless. I stared at her, unable to emit a sound. To me her demand was like the insidious slaps my father would give me when I was a child – punishments for crimes I hadn't committed. What could I say to her? There was such certainty in her voice that any reply would have rung hollow. She got up and left the room. That was the last time we shared a bed. Mina was not the kind of woman to go around the streets screaming about her missing child, pawing at her face in pain. She wouldn't have discussed it with her friends who came to drink tea at our house in the afternoon. The maids would occasionally catch her sighing in the kitchen, ranting to herself: "Where is my boy?"; "He must be freezing in this weather, wherever he is"; "He would have loved this . . ." Over the following twenty years, Mina continued to hope for a miracle. She was convinced her missing boy would just reappear one morning. She longed for him to drum on the door. In the old days, the moment she heard his familiar knock, she would jump up, quickly arrange her hair and rush out of the kitchen to open the door. She didn't just throw her arms around him, like any other mother would; she took time to admire the vision filling the entrance: her masterpiece, her achievement, her source of boundless pride, a handful of clay she had fashioned into a living statue – a loving, luminous, majestic tower of a man. She admired her strapping officer with an artist's eyes, his elegance, his fine features, the way he strutted about in his uniform. Abel couldn't resist lifting his mother up in the air and squeezing her in his arms. They would stay wrapped around each other for a moment – Mina birdlike and petite, Abel a hulk – not speaking, barely breathing, like two lovers who had been separated for months. Then he would put her down, bow and kiss her on the palm of her hand and then on the knuckles. A tender habit he'd had since childhood. She kept her hand stretched out and he willingly held on to it. Together, they walked to the sitting room. Abel knew he wouldn't escape an interrogation. Mina wanted to know all about his barracks, his trips to the Sahara, where the threat of war was greatest, and his next military parade, to which she would certainly invite her friends so they could admire her hero, too.

In truth, her nosiness was driven by one burning question: was Abel in love? She would casually steer conversation towards this subject. He could see her coming a mile away and simply grinned. But, seriously, did he have his sights set on a young woman? Was he smitten? He could confide in her. She wouldn't tell a soul. She knew how to keep a secret, but he had to tell her everything, right down to the last detail. Come on, what's her name? Go on, tell me. What does she look like? Where's she from? When he didn't reply, or simply avoided her questions, she became more and more insistent: heavens, when I was your age, I already had three children, twenty-five is old. It really is time you thought about getting married. All he had to do was give her the go-ahead and she would happily sort it out. There were many girls from good families in the neighbourhood, each prettier than the last. They would all be fighting over him, he was such a catch. Abel just had to give her a little nod and the whole matter would be settled in an instant. Then she switched to her sad voice: he had no right to deprive his ageing mother of grandchildren. Time was catching up with her and she didn't want to leave this world without meeting them. Anyway, what better gift could a son grant his mother than a sweet and charming daughter-in-law to keep her company, to lend a hand around the house. Soldiers are always on the road and a solid mother and daughter-in-law duo at home would make everyone happy.

Military leave was sporadic and Mina seemed determined not to waste a second of her son's visits. She would get down to the task of cooking Abel's favourite dishes: artichoke tagine with bitter olives and confit lemons, stuffed pigeon wrapped in thin pastry, barley couscous with seven vegetables . . . each day a different dish, exquisite flavours prepared with love. She wouldn't let anyone cook for her. The maids were in a state of high excitement whenever the young officer was in the house. One girl paced up and down the courtyard, shaking her backside as she mopped. The other rushed to water the thirsty orange trees in front of the living room. Then they'd exchange conspiratorial glances and blush as they spotted Abel sitting there, reading a book, bare-chested, a cigarette in the corner of his mouth. The maids were, of course, in love. They probably weren't the only ones. Mina pretended not to notice, though she was aware of their tricks. She secretly smiled about it, knowing that at their age her heart would have been churning in the same way. So she'd ask them to take her son a drink. Normally they had to be prodded into action, but they would argue about who could serve the Adonis his coffee. During Abel's short visits the kitchens ran on all cylinders as the stacks of plastic boxes he took back to his barracks were crammed with gazelle-horn biscuits, brique pastries with honey and almonds, and countless other handy snacks.

I can tell you all this in total freedom, without risking any breach in confidentiality. Tomorrow, or the day after tomorrow, Sidi will meet his maker and I will return to my family again. To you, Mina. I hope you will grant me the favour of hearing me out, without racing to conclusions. I would like to unburden my heart, not just quench the bitterness in yours. I want to try to make sense of our story. I am a man of faith, as you know. I swear by The Almighty that I never knew whether Abel was alive or dead. Nor did I know the name of the jail where he'd been sent to rot. All those unfair accusations of yours, as well as the contempt and hatred of others, crushed me. I suffered from the constant strain of it. I never complained: however hard it was, I knew it would have been unseemly to compare my pain to yours. Of course, I was aware, right away, that my role within the palace hierarchy meant that I should have been privy to state secrets, but none of you ever stopped to consider for a minute that someone in my perilous position – a father whose son had tried to assassinate the king – had no leeway at all. How can I explain to you, my love, that all those official statements I released were designed solely to protect the rest of our family? What choice did I have, other than to disown my own flesh and blood, to repudiate our son publicly, loudly and clearly? I had to cut every thread that bound me to the man who'd attempted to take my master's life. Oh, Mina! I'm asking for forgiveness. Forgiveness for having loved you in my noisy, clumsy and exhausting way. I'm sorry if I replicated a version of the palace in our own home, like a kinglet with his miniature court of toadies, dreamers and scroungers – people of little value, but whose triviality helped me accept life's trials. I'm sorry to have banned my son's name in our home, to have forbidden all reference to his troubled and destructive existence. Do you think I never noticed a thing? That the frenzy of court life prevented me from understanding what was happening to you? Do you think I didn't spot the pain tearing your angelic face apart? Mina, I could see your big eyes sinking into their sockets as if they were wells of sadness. I saw the wrinkles deepening on your face like

sentences of a book I hadn't wanted to write. I had no way
of curing the disease gnawing away at you. Your absent son
was more present in your heart than all of us put together.
Before each meal you would set a plate aside for him, in case
he appeared out of the blue and requested to be fed – just
like the old days, when he'd come back ravenous from the
barracks, and you'd watch him devour the meal you'd taken
hours to prepare in a few minutes flat. The "missing person's plate", as you called it, would pile up with more food,
the more you were consumed by yearning for your son, the
more unbearable his absence became. The maids would
feast on that plate daily as no-one ever came to claim it. I'm
sorry I became so caught up in the vanity of my duties at the
palace, and that I fell for all the role-playing. I thought it
would last for ever, but in the end it was just a game. We
were overindulged men behaving like children, driven by
puerile bickering and jealousy, by whims and fickleness. We
were children, in every way, except for our lost innocence.

No, I didn't want to revisit this pain. What's the point
of picking at this unhealed scab after all these years, stirring
the pits of the past to bring up our grudges and misery – all
the slough of former misunderstandings? What's the point of
returning to such indelible matters at our age? Haven't we
suffered enough? I guessed it would be near impossible for
me to shy away from this painful episode of our life. Sooner
or later, I knew I would be held responsible for things that
were not of my doing. Coward, you say? Perhaps you are
right. I could have chosen to walk out of that palace: others
had done so before me. I could have returned to normal life

and learned to walk amongst mere mortals again. I could have given up on glory, on having ordinary people bow to me, on the splendour of royal ceremonies and the dizzying pride of life amid the powerful, surrounded by jewels, gems and magnificence, a world founded on the erasure of all forms of ugliness. I could have gone back to Marrakesh, taught in any old school in the medina and tried to live with you as happily as possible. Maybe. But I'd already tasted the high life, seen the lavishness of power. My father said the poor cannot conceive of such a world. Their imagination can't see beyond the first gilt door. Otherwise they would rise up in fury.

My love, when will you stop accusing me of having stolen your son? I understand that he was only a young officer who obeyed his superiors' orders. He wasn't to know that the generals wanted to assassinate the king. Yet he can't have ignored the fact that his father was there in the palace that day as the soldiers went on the rampage, firing in all directions. Let's not dwell on this story any longer, as it tortures me every time.

9

THEY SAY THAT ANGELS grant the seriously ill a reprieve before the end, a miracle of borrowed time on the edge of the precipice. They say hope unsheathes its claws and clings on. I'm not so sure. I put Sidi's revival down to our impassioned prayers. We'd been beseeching God to spare our master for months, to ease his suffering. Our prayers had been answered. That was all.

Monsieur Brek, the chamberlain, dispatched an envoy early one morning with some highly surprising news: "Sidi is ready to play golf. Your presence is required." Remission from pain is one thing. Playing sport when you can barely stand is another. If Brek had had even the slightest hint of humour I would have thought it was some kind of tasteless joke. He was, however, the dourest person in the kingdom. I'm not exaggerating. There was no better proof of this than his face, a network of deep wrinkles etched into a permanent frown, as if he'd just swallowed a very bitter concoction. The herbalist, who wasn't known for his meanness, said Brek's face looked like a rough draft that had yet to be copied out in neat. According to him, the chamberlain and Boudda the dwarf were examples of God botching up His creations

– quite a broad category, incidentally. In the antechamber, I enjoyed studying the intricacy of Brek's unfinished face, where gullies and ravines fed into one another, running deeper and deeper until they formed a sealed maze of dead ends and loops. Bilal, the fortune-teller, seemed as fascinated by it as I was. Presumably, he could read the story of mankind in that face – its wars, tidal waves, plagues and genocides. The chamberlain's wrinkles clustered on his wide forehead, especially between his eyebrows, giving him the look of an emaciated, solitary lion. They then skirted around his eyes and fanned into crow's feet that seeped into the bulges of his crumpled cheeks like two dry figs. From there they followed the course of streaming tears into the corners of his mouth, tugging them into a downward sneer, before finally coming to rest in the pleat of his unappealing cleft chin. The overall impression was of a creased rag where sadness had staked out a permanent territory. It amazed me how Sidi managed to keep such a scowling man in his service. It was said that, being pathologically superstitious, the ruling family liked to surround themselves with monstrosity to ward off the evil eye: the belief being that bad luck wouldn't settle into a home where disaster was rife. Anyway, it wasn't that he was so absolutely hideous, it was more that his features, scattered onto an otherwise dull, oval face, gave off a kind of fluid sourness – bilious and repellent. If I ran into him in the morning I knew my day would take a turn for the worse. I teased him in private, out of earshot of the other courtiers, who just pestered him whenever they could. I preferred to rib him alone, with the king as sole witness.

That morning, when Sidi appeared all dressed up for golf, with the doughty Brek in tow, I couldn't believe my eyes, but I refused to show it. The slaves had barely come to the end of their tedious singsong praise before I got stuck in:

"Oh, Monsieur Brek, here you are at last," I said, while I kissed the king's hand.

The chamberlain looked at me suspiciously.

"I have a favour to ask you."

"I'm listening," he said almost tearfully.

Sidi settled into his armchair, expecting a sneaky ambush. He knew a joke was in the offing.

"I've thought long and hard before asking for your help, but no-one else but you can get me out of trouble."

"What can I do for you, my friend?"

"We've known each other for many years . . ."

"Indeed," Monsieur Brek said.

"I've never asked anything of you, have I?"

"Come on, get to the point. What's this about?"

"I won't be offended if my request doesn't meet with your approval. You see, I've just lost a very dear friend. He was like a brother to me."

"May he rest in peace," the chamberlain said, his face even more rumpled than usual.

"I'm due to attend his funeral this afternoon . . . and I don't know how to say this . . . I would like . . . as long as you agree, of course . . . to borrow your face to pay my respects to his family . . . As God, in his great mercy, endowed you with the perfect features for these occasions."

If the king hadn't guffawed the chamberlain would surely

have killed me on the spot. And because Sidi's mirth protected me, Monsieur Brek had no choice but to grace me with one of those hideous smirks he employed in lieu of a smile.

Despite having woken up in a relatively positive frame of mind, Sidi's moods continued to be unstable. He was liable to flip at any moment, as Moha's bent forefinger had rightly predicted. I was wary, therefore, as I settled into the front passenger seat of the king's vast car. He had decided to drive himself and we were heading for the golf course, a rather alpine-looking landscape in the distance. After the forest of maples and eucalyptus that ringed the palace, we reached the embassy district, crossed a bridge and found ourselves at the entrance to a magical place where I loved to walk with my master.

"Praise be the Lord."

The king looked at me, startled.

"What's got into you?"

"Nothing, Your Majesty. I'm thanking God, that's all. Isn't this an astounding sight? The poor boy from the medina in the most luxurious British car driven by none other than the king himself. It's a fantasy gone mad, Sidi!"

The king smiled.

"But why me, Your Majesty?"

"Because you were born lucky, 'on a white sheet' as we like to say. Your parents blessed you. You're a good man, Mohamed."

When you come from Marrakesh's overcrowded medina, such endless expanses of uninhabited greenery make you feel as if you've set foot in the paradise they banged on about at Qur'anic school. Stretches of clipped lawn roll into gentle hillocks, before straddling ponds and fading into a horizon where sea and blue sky merge. Strange triangular flags flutter in the wind, the territorial markings of the international big-bucks brigade. Miniature cars, like children's toys, ferry couples dressed in white from head to toe, their skin slightly flushed despite their baseball caps, and they automatically exchange waves and smiles whenever another little vehicle crosses their path.

We had arrived at the V.I.P. lounge. A swarm of ministers scrambled to their feet and began bowing while we were still a good ten metres away. Sidi brushed them aside with a flick of his hand and reached the green where his caddie awaited. The bigwigs dispersed in as dignified a manner as possible: some to the bar, others to the pool house, others still to the terrace overlooking the driving range. Had this cast of characters got wind of Moha's bent forefinger, they would have slipped away as quietly as possible, forgetting the signature they so desperately needed for their paperwork, and without which nothing was possible. Sidi's poor health was hampering the smooth running of the entire kingdom. Many pressing issues remained worryingly unresolved. I could tell how concerned the ministers were from their sudden friendliness towards me. They flattered me, forgetting that gushing praise was my currency. They promised me the moon – me, of all people, the biggest bigmouth at court. They knew my knack for resolving intractable problems and cornered me: I had to sweet-talk the boss into signing papers that could no longer wait. To some of them I was a kind of saviour, to others a future martyr. I was completely aware of that. Indeed, I must have seemed like both. The role of messenger, it is well known, is not without occupational hazards.

There is no such thing as immunity in the royal palace. No-one is safe from sanction. I'd often been needed in moments of crisis and managed to get out of them unscathed, but I, like everyone else, had ended up being punished. My ostracism lasted several months and was the bleakest period of my career, of my life, in fact. The dishonour that befell some of my companions, and which I've described to you, was nothing compared to my downfall. For good reason. I was punished for another man's transgression – my son's, as it so happened. The harsh penalty fell the day after the failed *coup d'état* – when the shadow of treason clung to me. I remember that cursed day when Monsieur Brek took me by the arm and drew me away from the other courtiers. He led me to his office next to Sidi's quarters. The room was like the chamberlain himself, covered from ceiling to floor in fine wood and as cold as it was impersonal, like a military court. An obsessively tidied desk stood between us: not a paper, not a single folder, cluttered its polished surface. Monsieur Brek spoke in a soft voice: "You do know how fond I am of you, Mohamed? If I had to keep one courtier, it would be you, without doubt. Hard to believe, isn't it? Words are not really my thing and yet I have more humour than you give me credit for. You're a good person, Mohamed. I knew it the moment you entered this palace. The current turmoil will eventually fade. It has to. We all know you had nothing to do with this. If you'd had wind of it in any way, you would have called in sick the night before the massacre. But no, you witnessed the slaughter with the rest of us. You risked your life like everyone else. History will be kind to you: I saw how death breathed over us, together. How will we ever forget that poky basement room where we remained holed up for hours, huddled around Sidi, as those barbaric and relentless gunshots echoed through the rooms upstairs? I saw you tremble, Mohamed, just as I saw the king looking distraught, staring emptily, while we mumbled verses of the Qur'an. Understanding that Sidi was losing heart, and not able to think straight, you found a way to bring him back to reality:

'Your Majesty?' you said.

'The kings are those machine-gunning us down,' he replied.

'Before I die, I'd like one last wish . . .'

'Talk to the insurgents, Mohamed. Your monarch can no longer do anything for you.'

'They'll listen to you, Your Majesty. Everyone listens to a king. Before they kill me, tell them to avoid shooting my head. None of this was caused by my head. Let them fire their ammunition into my fat, hungry stomach, the true culprit in my life, and in all this. It is never fully sated and deserves to be blown to smithereens. It was probably this stomach of mine that led us to this cursed basement where we're all cornered like rats.'

"I have no idea if the king's laugh was nervous or not, but he smirked loudly, setting off a wave of panic amongst our group as we could have been heard. A short while later, as if brought back to his senses, Sidi decided to lead us out of our hideout, against the advice of one of the officers. But that is what saved us.

"You see you worked to the bitter end. I'm convinced you rescued us. Be patient, Mohamed. Let this storm pass. You've been wanting a break for a while. This is your moment. Don't return to the palace over the next few days. Go home, enjoy spending time with the two children you still have. We'll call you when we need you, I promise. Sidi is still shaken by this awful crisis. He doesn't want to see you for the time being – actually, he doesn't want to see many people."

In spite of our many squabbles, the sadness in Monsieur Brek's eyes seemed genuine. His soothing words rang true though they brought me no consolation. Something in the bond between my master and me had been irreparably damaged and it caused me no end of suffering. Such is suspicion. A poison like no other.

Do you remember that evening, Mina? I came home unusually early. You took one glance at my haggard face and realised something was up. You didn't ask any questions. You dismissed the maids and served dinner yourself to avoid any disturbance or noise. You made me drink some soup. I wasn't hungry. I behaved like a spoiled child, yet you didn't tell me off – or only half-heartedly. You said: "You seem very tired. Come, let's go upstairs, I'll take care of you." I loved the soft whispering of your promises when you felt the need to pamper me. Up in the bedroom, you filled a bowl of water and scented it with orange flowers, adding just enough salt, and you made me dip my feet into it. My eyes shut, I felt the kindness of your fingers stroking my skin, tugging at my toes, kneading the spots you knew required attention and it relaxed me enormously. A splurge of water drenched us when you brushed your hand across the soles of my feet. I am very ticklish, as you knew so well. You deliberately caused all that splashing, didn't you, my love? We mucked around, dowsing each other in water. I protected myself, as best I could, fought back, enjoying wetting your silk caftan. The sudden appearance of your sublime breasts kindled a desire in me. Two almost ripe pears pierced through the thin fabric clinging to your skin. Soaked to the bone, we laughed like little fiends who had been given the power to breathe joy into a carcass of sorrow. We were sad, thoroughly miserable. You bit me hard as we made love. I didn't cry out. I enjoyed your bites. I liked your tooth marks on my skin, your fury, your cravings, the suppressed violence in you, those private, possessive grievances of yours. You wanted me to yourself. Undivided. Free from the chains of servitude I had tethered to my ankle all my life. You wanted me without the usual phoniness, to keep my jokes and poetry for yourself. It was time to laugh for laughter's sake, to sing for the sake of singing, to enjoy a love that was accountable to no-one else but us. You wanted to free me, my dearest love. You communicated with me like a deaf person, with burning eyes and shaky hands: your heart and guts bent on reviving our long-lost blessings. Do you remember the white sheet you wrapped and dried me in? I was an abandoned body, sated with pleasure, drained of life. Without you knowing it, you had sent me back to my childhood, to a time when, refusing to entrust me to my father, my mother would bundle me up in a bathrobe and sneak me into the women's hammam. She would settle me down in a dark corner and scrub me from head to toe. I was her swaddled, ten-year-old baby, awestruck and bewitched by the profusion of differently shaped women bustling around me: saggy breasts slid onto fat stomachs, pert bosoms adorned skinny bodies, bushy tufts and little trimmed beards appeared between legs, though some had no hair at all. Women with luscious mouths laughed, yelled and hurled insults while many remained silent, lips shut tight. And everywhere water poured over quivering buttocks, cascaded down long tresses thick with black soap and *ghassoul* clay, or swelled into a rivulet carrying hairs of different lengths and colours . . . I always regretted leaving the sweltering duskiness of the hammam with its circus of bodies and fantasies. At the first sign of any complaint, the slightest hostile glare, my mother would roll me back up in my bathrobe, depriving me of the magical show, and carry me to the rest area, where they sold fresh water at great expense. My love, you could have been the wife of any one of the courtiers in the royal household. Although we didn't choose each other, we quickly accepted each other. Now, I can state it openly, loud and clear, to God and my fellow men: you have been the most beautiful part of my life.

That first night of my disgrace felt like a homecoming. I understood that my empire had been built on sand, yet you had the grace to spare me the speeches I didn't want to hear. I needed kindness and you overwhelmed me with it. You burned incense in a dish and then slipped into our bed. You positioned a pillow behind me to soften the pain in my back and put your arms around me. You stroked my hair the way my mother used to when I was little, to ward off the monsters haunting my nights. I dozed off, my ear against your beating heart.

But let's get back to that golf trip and how I was escorting my newly revived master through the immense V.I.P. lounge, with all the ministers and high-ranking officers staring at me the way one might view a life-raft in the midst of a rough sea. I had decided to throw myself into the waves to pull Sidi out of his daze, to help him see it was worth talking to the ministers. A tricky task as first I had to work on his temper, which frayed further every time he missed a shot on the golf course. He had never been particularly gifted at the sport, but now he was physically incapacitated, too. Accosting him in such circumstances involved appreciable risk. My long career at court, however, had taught me to trust my instincts, to listen to the spirits whispering gags in my ear, to improvise, dare and surprise. I followed Sidi from afar, waiting for an idea to drop into my lap. It wasn't easy to quicken my pace on the golf course dressed in a djellaba and a pair of babouches. All the same, I managed to catch up with the king on a square patch of lawn that had been mown shorter than the rest. A hole lay ahead of him next to a caddie tending the royal flag. Sidi pretended not to notice me, fully concentrating on getting his putt right. I held my breath as he chipped the ball. The beast evidently had a mind of its own, and was intent on making my life more difficult, as it rolled down a slope, a good ten metres from its intended destination. Sidi scowled and hurled his club onto the grass. I began to clap as loudly as I could, and nod my head at the same time. Sidi glared at me.

"Well done," I said. "Really well done."

"Are you teasing me?"

"Not in the slightest, Your Majesty."

"Didn't you see that my shot was woefully off target?"

"No, Sidi, you didn't miss anything. The hole wasn't in the right place, that's all. Those who dug it should be whipped, to set an example."

It was the last time I ever saw Sidi bent over with laughter.

Back in the V.I.P. lounge, he sat at a table and the ministers lined up, one after the other, like schoolboys, to hand him their documents. He signed the lot without bothering to read a word.

BILAL HAD MADE IT a rule not to divulge forthcoming disasters. Even if his cards hinted at something calamitous, he carried on laying them out without losing his composure. His closed face revealed no emotion. His pupils, wrinkles, eyelashes and lips didn't budge: nothing would help you decipher the cards' hidden message. You were deluding yourself, too, if you thought you could tease anything out of him . . . He would, however, willingly dispense other forms of divination in exchange for a token coin. Even Sidi had to abide by this rule despite the fact he didn't encumber his royal person with bits of loose change. We would quarrel over who would offer the king a coin, which he often returned a hundredfold or more. Yet the evening Saher asked to consult Bilal, because he was worried about his mother's health, the fortune-teller flatly refused, claiming he had an appalling migraine. Oddly, this unusual occurrence didn't alarm us. We should have known better. Such a refusal didn't bode well.

My master's personality irrevocably changed with the wild adventure of the "Green March". There are decisions that no man would ever want to take. Sending hundreds of thousands of citizens on a march south to conquer the desert, armed only with budget Qur'ans and faded flags, would rattle most people, however resilient. You don't come out of such an experience unscathed. Even more so when you're at the helm of a ship crammed with good-for-nothings crippled by genetic laziness. My position at court meant that I had first-hand experience of this historical event and the way it altered the nature of our country. Preparations for it kept my master busy night and day. He lived, thought and breathed this grand enterprise, from its beginnings as an idea to the fully fledged plan that thrilled the whole kingdom. Thanks to it, ordinary men and women suddenly felt duty-bound to become the guardians of stretches of desert they barely knew or had never even heard of before. They began to dream of grains of sand, of a breast-like dune adorned with a nomadic tribesman's tent, a fearless camel caught in a beam of blinding sunlight.

The excitement sent the country into a spin: airwaves, towns and homes were filled with patriotic songs. Euphoric artists took to the streets and public squares to serve the country, blinkers firmly attached. Their creativity had but one aim: to underline the desert's historical relevance to the national psyche. It was a matter of state importance. All media outlets spoke with one voice – stoking the rabble's jingoistic longing to reclaim the desert provinces of the South. A new, thrilling mood surged through villages and cities, where lamp posts decked with Sidi's giant portrait soon cast longer shadows than the plane trees of the big boulevards. And the crowds became ever more fervent at the sight of streams of requisitioned cars and coaches. Queues of jubilant volunteers stretched round railway and bus stations while ancient, clapped-out trucks held up the traffic in outskirts and suburbs. A tide of peasants spilled into the cities and littered the pavements, avenues and parks with filthy blankets to sleep in the starlit breeze of the night. The gateways to the South had recovered their old dignity and splendour: those glorious days when gold, sugar and spices passed through them had returned. Men and women gave up on sleep. The hurly-burly of daytime merged with the racket of night. The risky gamble my master had devised was about to kick off. The sheer scale of it, considered and reconsidered, time and time again, had him worried sick. He'd evaluated every little detail of the preparations, followed the operations closely. He no longer slept, no longer ate, smoked one cigar after another, poisoned himself with endless coffees and spent hours on the telephone speaking a whole gamut of languages. His plan was the work of either a genius or of a madman – only time would tell. But what was done was done and he had to see it through. The optimism of the first days gave way to dark fears: what if the humiliated Spanish colonial army shot at the marching crowds . . . ? Such an outcome couldn't be discounted. Sidi would then be held responsible for the atrocious massacre. Men and women, who had come from all corners of Morocco, ordinary people who had been led into believing the integrity of their country was at stake, would have died answering their king's call to action.

A few days before the Green March, as we were drinking tea together in the courtyard, Sidi said the following, and it was unlike anything I'd ever heard him utter before: "If this 'great march' screws up we'll have no choice but to pack up our bags and leave." I still don't know if the king was talking to himself or to me, his faithful servant. It didn't matter. In my panicked mind, I saw myself on a road, heading north, carrying my master's suitcase on top of mine, both of us fleeing the retribution of the angry masses. I walked behind Sidi, head bowed, running the gauntlet of men and women who spat and hurled insults and stones at us.

That I even had such thoughts sums up the king's spirits during that period, and why his fasting increasingly worried us. We hoped for a miracle at every meal. Yet Moha would leave the king's quarters with a scowl on his face, his trolley of food as untouched as it had been when he wheeled it in. The king hadn't emerged in three days. He was refusing to see anyone. Shut up in his office, he kept his anguish and worries from us, his dread, too – but we were paid for the bad times as much as the good.

A strange silence filled the antechamber. Bilal consulted his cards, as usual, while the herbalist topped up his silver dish with incense, mumbling obscure spells. Frustrated at not being able to irritate anyone, Boudda lashed out at the stony-faced minders on the door. Dr Mourra, who viewed his fellow humans as clusters of ducts, blood vessels, fat and muscle, read a medical textbook and kept an eye on Saher. The musician had been unwell, complaining of pains in his left arm, and was stretched out in a corner of the room. As for me, I was wondering how I might rouse Sidi from his self-imposed confinement. The queen mother, Lalla Oum

Sidi, summoned me, and I hurried to her apartments in the southern wing of the palace. I was as fond of this fine lady as she was of me.

"Your king hasn't eaten anything in three days," she said.

"I know, Lalla."

"Well what's the point of you, Mohamed, if you can't do something about it?"

"He doesn't want to see anyone."

"That's irrelevant and you know it. We expect miracles of men with your skills. Come on, wake up. Put your thinking cap on."

"I'm trying my best, Lalla."

"This march of the people isn't going to come to anything if your king hasn't eaten. His fasting could jeopardise the whole thing."

"Sidi is threatening to punish anyone who defies his instructions. He's not letting us in."

Lalla tried to catch my eye, but I averted my gaze.

"Look at me, Mohamed. Find a way to get your master to eat. No-one, believe me, will touch a single hair on your head, or they'll have to whip me first."

Emboldened by Lalla's protection, I headed back to the gloomy antechamber, where the courtiers were still feeling as powerless as ever. I didn't bother glancing at the depressing sight of Monsieur Brek standing in the doorway, as stiff as ever, flanked by the equally gloomy Moha. They hadn't sat down all day. In fact, they had forbidden themselves from sitting down in case they were delayed by a fraction of a second when Sidi summoned them. From afar you couldn't distinguish one from the other: they wore the same neat clothes, their chests puffed out, their faces forlorn, the pair of them on heightened alert as if some unknown enemy were about to burst into the corridor and harm the monarch. Brek and Moha understood each other, worked in complete synergy, like twins. If my mother had met them on the back-streets of the medina she would surely have said: "A slappable face always gets the slap it deserves." I used to laugh at that expression, as she meant that one blow invariably invites another, and that bad luck always attracts more bad luck. So the "slappable face" and the "slap" lived together in perfect harmony, the king's happiness their goal and *raison d'être*.

Stuck in the antechamber, with the television blaring, I couldn't escape the onslaught of propaganda as our trusty old state channel relayed the news it was permitted to relay: the people of Morocco had flocked together, en masse, Qur'an in one hand, flag in the other, to await the king's orders . . .

I stood up and asked to talk to Sidi. Moha tried to gauge my level of determination, to understand how much I'd really thought about my decision, to check I was fully aware of the risks. Seeing my resoluteness, he shouted my name.

Sidi refused to let me in: "Give him what he wants and send him away."

"I just need two minutes of my master's time," I said.

It was a good half-hour before the king let me enter.

"You'd do anything to distinguish yourself from your companions, wouldn't you?" he grumbled. "Don't you see I'm in no mood for jesting?"

"But, Your Majesty, I'm not here to make you laugh.

It's my stomach, yet again, that's going to get me whipped a hundred times. It's beyond me, I can't help it."

"What has your fat belly got to do with anything?"

"Your Majesty, I've been begging someone to cook me a dried-camel-meat tagine for three days – you know, the one they slow-cook in salted fat with spiced tomatoes and soft-boiled eggs. Not a single charitable soul in the royal kitchens is taking my needs seriously. It's a violation of my culinary rights. I discovered the wonders of this dish right here, nowhere else. I feel like a pregnant woman with cravings. This is an urgent matter, Sidi. You have to save me."

The king smiled and gestured to Moha.

"Bring some *khlii* tagine to the Fqih. I wouldn't want the child he's carrying to be scarred by malnutrition."

Ten minutes later, Moha's lanky figure appeared pushing a trolley of food. One hand stuck to his telephone receiver, the other supporting his grimacing face, Sidi was still arguing with important people on the other end of the line. When Moha lifted the silver bell from the food, and a delicious aroma wafted through the room, I put my hands together like the Christians do and gave thanks to God for the heavenly feast before me. I dunked a piece of warm bread into the runny egg yolk and then stripped off a dried and perfectly salted piece of meat.

"Who cares about cholesterol?" I exclaimed. "It's just made up by people who have no taste buds."

I raised my eyes as I ate my second mouthful and hurled some perfectly legitimate insults at Dr Mourra, who had had the nerve to forbid me from eating bread because of my diabetes, salt because of my high blood pressure and meat because of my gout-like symptoms. If I'd listened to that killjoy I would have long been buried. I crammed some more cholesterol – sprinkled with diabetes and seasoned with a pinch of high blood pressure – into my mouth. I savoured the dish in a state of manifest ecstasy. My master watched me out of the corner of his eye.

At the first available lull, the moment the telephone stopped ringing, Sidi walked over to me, to my plate, in point of fact, grabbed a chunk of succulent meat and stuffed it in his mouth. He reached for another piece and wolfed it down, too. After that he snatched my bread and, in a few minutes, gobbled up the whole tagine. He licked the bowl clean, from rim to rim, almost forgetting my presence. Seeing my master give up on his jittery fast pleased me no end. He let himself drop back onto the sofa and let out a huge sigh in which the collective gratitude of Christians, Muslims and Jews was mingled . . . in fact, the praise of all starved beings who have finally been given a scrap of bread dipped in fat. My mission accomplished, I stood to take my leave.

"You're not going anywhere," he said.

"Whatever you say, Your Majesty."

"We're leaving in an hour."

I nodded.

That evening we flew to Agadir. From there, in the middle of the night, the king launched the Green March.

I'LL ADMIT IT, I'M superstitious. Like it or not, there are coincidences that can't be coincidental, just as there are happy endings and weird connections that feel as if they've been engineered by the Heavens and artful angels. And what of conspiracies apparently whipped up by evil spirits, or revenge that has more than an element of poetic justice about it? We know nothing about so many things. Secrets stare us in the face. We just don't see them.

When misfortune strikes, I have a miraculous trick, a form of ancient poetry that protects me. As the world threatens to crumble around me, light turning to gloom, I recite the *Munfarija*. The clouds soon part and my distress lifts.

So what is this magic spell that can cancel out pain so effectively? The *Munfarija* is the masterwork of a poet and jeweller who lived in the fifth century of the Hegira. He was courtier to a particularly bloody king of the Almoravid dynasty. By the way, it's perfectly possible to be both a jeweller and a poet. The two aren't at odds. Quite the opposite. Both professions require the handling of gems, a honing of pearls or precious words, not to mention finding the perfect setting to stir the emotions. Anyway, our court poet, who went by the name of Abou Fadl, composed a poem on what was supposed to be his last night on earth. My father recounted this story towards the end of his life as if he were handing me a charm to ward off bad luck. This is what he told me:

The night before his wife was about to give birth, the king presented the jeweller with an emerald the size of a muscat grape, pristine and astonishingly pure. The intensity of its greenness, its glimmer and radiance, altered with every fluctuation in the sunlight. The poet studied it with the eyes of a jeweller and the jeweller with the eyes of a poet. And in the eyes of both, the world suddenly seemed more luminous, shimmering and miraculous.

The king wanted as inconspicuous a mount as possible, to bring out the true majesty of the emerald, to draw attention to its almost imperceptible fissures, which are charmingly named its "gardens". It was an absolute wonder of a stone. The king had sent for it from a far-flung corner of eastern Egypt. He was all the more delighted to be gifting it to his wife as the fortune-tellers had predicted, thanks to their dreams and crystal balls, that she would give birth to a boy. He had to welcome this new crown prince in style.

Abou Fadl locked himself away in his workshop with the precious stone, lit the oil lamps, laid out his tools, put his glasses on and set about his task with as much spirit and urgency as he could muster. The king was expecting the ring to be set and ready by the following morning, without fail. But, as my father liked to say, "Boats never sail in the direction the wind wants to take them." Sometimes disaster singles you out, malevolent stars align and darkness comes to toy with you. Abou Fadl had just begun crafting the stone when it cracked in two. Without warning. It seemed impossible that a solid gemstone could just break. He stared at the catastrophe before him in a state of numbness and shock. The king had been so proud of the gift he was about to give his graceful wife for the birth of their prince: an emerald like no other, dug up from the wildernesses of the desert. Now the jeweller had ruined their celebration. How would he even begin to tell the king? He knew what his punishment would be, of that he had no doubt: he would be dragged off to the scaffold. What excuse could he possibly come up with? Incompetence? Absent-mindedness? There was no way out. Upsetting the king in this way warranted death: Abou Fadl knew that all too well. He spent a good part of the night in his workshop, his weary head bowed, whining and scratching at his face like those women who are paid to mourn and wail at funerals. Realising how hopeless the situation was, the poet in him took over from the despairing jeweller and tried to provide some comfort. He chose his most delicate and supple quill and dipped it in ink and wrote the finest poem any man or woman, born of flesh and blood, has ever addressed to God. This is how the *Munfarija* was born: a miracle of literature, written with grace and dignity, with the choked tears of a cornered man begging his Maker not to abandon him. The tender poem, with just the right dosage of humility and passion, was heard by the Heavens. Whatever people say, God appreciates genius.

As dawn broke, Abou Fadl was pulled from his stupor

by a series of violent knocks at his door. He opened it to discover the vizier himself, on his white steed, flanked by guards.

"Bad news, Abou Fadl!"

"You know, My Lord?"

"About what?"

"About the emerald," he said, shaking.

"Absolutely. I've come to tell you to start all over again. God, in His infinite grace, has granted His Majesty twins, a boy and a girl. The king would like you to produce two identical rings, not one. He advises you to split the emerald in two. The jewels have to be delivered by eight o'clock this evening, on the dot."

"It will be my pleasure, Your Excellency. I'll return to my workshop straightaway. Thank you, sir. Praise be to God."

That is how the poet saved the jeweller – and the vizier couldn't help but smile at the total unpredictability of artists.

So the *Munfarija* became my lucky poem. I recited it often and each time its dignified lament moved me. It would be too long and tedious to list all the times this magical text has got me out of a tight corner. There were certainly occasions when Abou Fadl's troubles seemed to mirror my own. Despite the centuries separating them, our kings shared a similar approach to authority. For a start, they didn't let qualms get in their way when they felt it necessary to chop off someone's head. To them, there was no difference between a man and an insect's life.

Saher would long remember a winter's night when we visited a mountain palace for the first time. Sidi had kept us back from our companions to help him get to sleep. While the musician strummed his oud, I kicked off with a joke a friend had told me the evening before. You'll soon understand how there's little chance of escape when the Heavens decide to pick on you: why on earth did I tell that joke rather than another? I have no idea. It was about an Andalusian king who had gathered his whole harem together, about fifty concubines of all ages. They congregated in the women's garden, and the king stood up and solemnly announced: "Ladies, I've brought you here today to give you some bad news. You'll doubtlessly hate me, but I can't hide my feelings anymore. I'm in love with another harem."

I couldn't tell whether the king chuckled at my story or at Saher, who rolled around on the floor in fits, snorting like a puppy. Quickly remembering he was in the king's presence, the musician picked up his oud and started playing again. I immediately followed up with a string of poems which required subtle and detailed commentary. I drew on the loves and sufferings of the artists who'd composed them, and explored the historical context of each work, merrily drifting off on tangents that Sidi, exhausted by a long day's work, found hard to follow. He tried to cling on, but he ended up falling asleep. At the first sound of snoring, I gestured to Saher to play more quietly, and we left the king's quarters on the top floor of that palace in the shadow of a snow-capped mountain. We got in the lift to return to our companions waiting for us in a large drawing room on the ground floor, huddled round an enormous fireplace where you could have happily roasted several chickens or a good-sized sheep – a proper spit-roast. Saher must have pressed the wrong button as the lift opened onto an unknown floor. We stupidly decided to get out, not realising that we had wandered onto the level reserved for His Majesty's concubines. Our blood curdled on hearing high-pitched voices and laughter from the nearby rooms. Yet when we turned back we were shocked to discover there was no button to open the lift again, nothing at all to save us from the mess we'd got ourselves into. We looked at each other in dismay. What would we tell the king if he found out about our incursion into the women's quarters? "We tucked you up in bed, Your Majesty, like a baby, and then slipped off to your harem!" That's how our reckless blunder would have been viewed. Saher crouched down, his oud resting between his knees. I squatted next to him, my mind in disarray, unable to think straight. The words of the *Munfarija* spontaneously sprung from my mouth like a prayer.

The harem is one of several taboos in the royal household. No-one had forgotten a terrible story from the time of the failed *coup d'état* when a group of soldiers managed to break into the women's quarters. Many of the women had been waiting, like us, to be gunned down that day. A mutineer, one of those lowlifes with eyes filled with bloodlust, walked up to a petrified concubine and lifted the hem of her caftan with his machine gun. He pointed the tip of it at her genitals and pretended to penetrate her. "So is this where your master stuffs his dick, you filthy bitch?" An outraged soldier stepped forward and pushed him to one side: "We don't attack women, you dog. Where's your honour? Get out or I'll deal with you right here."

The memory of this affront never faded in Sidi's mind. He spoke of his need for revenge all the time – a king bothered by an insect. He would have given his fortune to find the bastard who had humiliated him, to punish the soldier as only he knew how. Sidi's many investigations invariably led him to the death jails in the South, where my own son was rotting away. The soldier who saved the women was identified and brought to the king. I was in the room that night when the hulking and blindfolded man was dragged in by four guards. The soldier no doubt recognised the king's voice as he proposed a simple deal: "Give me the name of the bastard who mistreated my woman and I'll free you tonight."

The man insisted he had forgotten. He didn't give his brother-in-arms away and he was executed for it. I find such *esprit de corps* hard to understand, this willingness to die in order to spare another's life. Such solidarity doesn't exist in my world: we're capable of sacrificing a whole tribe to save ourselves.

This old wound, alone, would have been justification enough to send Saher and me to the gallows for violating the secret of the women's floor. I mumbled the *Munfarija* without realising that my voice, overcome by fear, had got louder and louder. A middle-aged lady I sometimes met in Sidi's quarters opened a door. Seeing us squatting near the lift, she looked at us in astonishment.

"What are you doing here, Mohamed?"

"Save us, please – we pressed the wrong button in the lift and now we don't know how to get out again."

She put a finger to her lips and beckoned us to follow

her. We dashed along a corridor which led to a back spiral staircase and raced down it like thieves. At the bottom she whispered something to a guard and he let us out without further fuss.

There you have the extraordinary power of the *Munfarija*. But even poetry has its limits.

Neither Bilal and his magic cards, nor Dr Mourra's legendary skills, nor even the herbalist who fended off the evil eye with his burning alum, were able to foresee the tragedy that hit us head-on, without warning, without allowing us to prepare for the unbearable, gaping hole it would leave – an absence which, I have to confess, I found crueller than that of my own son. Worried and drained by the king's failing health and repeated fasting, Dr Mourra didn't take Saher's ailments seriously. The musician had recurring aches and a numbness in his left arm, but, typically, he underplayed these. He almost apologised for causing a fuss. His dizzy spells didn't particularly worry the doctor either, and we put them down to fatigue. One evening, in the din of the lobby where we awaited the king's summons, Saher said his prayers and came and sat next to me. Our wives were neighbours and got on very well – in fact, they spent most of their time together. Saher said this friendship made him very happy, reassured him, even. I nodded and smiled, but he surprised me further by alluding to an old Muslim tradition that states that when a man dies it is recommended that his brother marry the widow to ensure the children are protected. This unwholesome custom actually rather repulsed me. It seemed distasteful that someone could legitimately fornicate with his sister-in-law like this. It was just another form of incest to me. Saher disagreed. He believed such a system worked. An uncle would necessarily feel more affection for his nieces and nephews than some new husband. The Prophet himself, he said, had recommended the advantages of the practice in a Hadith. After a short silence, Saher startled me even more by adding: "Don't forget, Mohamed, that we are brothers, you and I." The way he spoke, and the tone of his voice, made me uneasy: I could have sworn the shadow of the Grim Reaper was prowling around us at that very moment. To put an end to the futile conversation, I told Saher I had no intention of dying and I had even less intention of handing my wife over to another man. Saher barely smiled. He tried to tune his oud, gave up and then stood it on a carpet between two ottomans. He then took his shoes off, lay down on the sofa and died, there and then, without a single sound, just as he had lived, with the utmost discretion. He had left our lobby as quietly as he had tiptoed into it thirty years beforehand, an artist taking a silent bow at the end of a long career. We lost his art, his singing, his music and poetry, as well as his kindness and heartwarming smiles. We had been stripped of his truth, of the camaraderie he'd spent years trying to instil in us. I will blame the doctor until my dying day for having let him go without a fight, and the fortune-teller, too, for not having warned us of the tragedy a year earlier. I also blame myself for not questioning his sudden apathy, or why he grew increasingly tired of music. And I'm angry at the chamberlain for deciding to hide Saher's death from His Majesty, and at the courtiers for having agreed to this conspiracy of silence so as not to frighten the dying king. Saher deserved a state funeral and a whole lot more. The entire country should have mourned the death of such a pure, talented and generous being. There, I've said it. It was wrong to just ship the musician's body off to the village where he was born without any prayers or ceremony, without honours.

But I wasn't the sort of man to give up without a fight. Snug in his beige cashmere djellaba, in a foetal position, Saher looked as if he were asleep. How could death pose as sleep with such ease? Treacherous, thieving death! It always gets what it wants. I had a secret device to resuscitate my friend, however. I leaned towards his ear and recited the *Munfarija*, convinced I could rouse him from sleep, that he would sit up and grab his oud and once again bewitch us with his talent. I declaimed verse after verse, enunciating each syllable the way the imam of the palace mosque did when the king was in attendance. I was sure my words would be heard by God, and Saher would escape death's clutches and take flight again, up in the heavens, with the birds and other blessed beings, and with us in tow. Perhaps he would even allow us a glimpse of that celestial world that only artists and madmen see. We were ready to follow him, to venerate and praise him, too. I placed my hand on his cheek, then on his gently cooling forehead, and recited the miraculous poem with renewed determination. The *Munfarija* was bound to get a smile out of him, at the very least light up the gaze behind those thick glasses that magnified his pupils so grotesquely. His were open, startled eyes, brimming with vitality – which observed, loved, yearned and drifted, saw the darkness deep within all of us and then flitted back to daylight, horrified by life's hellish and inexplicable workings. Yet nothing happened. Saher didn't stir. However hard Dr Mourra pumped his chest, pushed him around, breathed into his mouth, he didn't react. It was over. That was it. Death is as idiotically simple as that. No-one can do anything about it. The *Munfarija* proved to be useless that day. It pathetically revealed its failings.

Strangely, Boudda the dwarf began to weep. No-one at court had ever seen him cry the way he did for Saher.

12

WHEN IT COMES TO her children, a mother, however old and wizened, however crippled and partially sighted, develops the sort of sixth sense that would turn a fortune-teller like Bilal green with envy. Twenty years after their disappearance, no sane person would have bet a dirham on seeing any of the mutineers return from the death holes of the Southern desert. Only Mina thought she would see her missing son again, that she would hold him in her arms once more, speak to him, shower him with the love she'd been holding back for years. At dinner, when she spoke of his impending return, the children and I would exchange pitying glances, not wanting to crush her fanciful thinking. Young Toufiq, in particular, asked lots of questions about his big brother as he had barely known him. Mina would sit up immediately, smooth the furrows of sadness on her face and, like a proud mother with a new baby, praise her son's beauty, his intelligence and exceptional sense of humour. She had never-ending stories about his childhood and youth, including his first years in the army. She would reel off episodes of his life that everyone had heard a thousand times, happily lose herself in exaggerated twists and digressions, on and on. Each story triggered a new sequence of stories, some true, some invented, and they flowed through her web of random references and fabrications. No-one cared as an undeniable truth had lit up her eyes.

And I was wrong all along! For all our shrewdness and far-sightedness we turned out to be mistaken, each and every one of us. We thought Mina was an old fantasist, who just wanted to delude herself, but we had to swallow our pride when the implausible occurred.

Despite her age and frailty, she heard a rapping at the door one day, like the beating of a drum. She instantly recognised the sound. She leaped from bed, heart beating, and rushed to look for her son's imposing silhouette in the doorway. There, between two policemen, supporting him on either side, she saw an old, hunched man, corpse-like in his gauntness, his face pitted, cheekbones jutting out beneath haggard eyes. This human rag, crushed by the mill of hatred and barbarity, could not stand unaided, but still he smiled at her, his teeth as saw-edged and crenellated as the walls of a castle. Mina studied the person she'd been delivered with suspicion, fearing a mistake. Yet the mole on the left dimple was exactly like her son's. She didn't quite trust her failing eyes. Abel was tall, well-built, an unstoppable force – this was a piece of cloth that seemed as if it had been shrunk in a boiling wash. How could muscles just wilt, fall away to leave nothing but bone and veins, like a tree that has surrendered to the desert sun? It was inconceivable. Though the moment the man opened his mouth she heard her son's voice: "It's me, Mother, it's me."

Mina scrunched up her eyes, leaned towards Abel and sniffed him like an animal. She didn't flinch, as any other mother might have done on seeing her son – or rather, what remained of him after twenty years of exile. She refused to yield, to let the voices in her head take over, even though they were beseeching her to roll in the dust, to bang her face against the floor and spew out the ancient, pent-up bitterness in her heart. Her ultimate act of resilience was to hold herself together. She didn't cave in. She'd spent two decades resisting the siren calls of grief, refusing the relief that would have come from casting off her burden and welcoming the abyss. She didn't let her knees give way, or allow her frail body to collapse. She was like a crumbling wall, a wall patched together with spit and mud, and with just enough strength to remain standing until God, overwhelmed by her prayers, finally fulfilled her wish to see her son again. The two humbled policemen propped Abel up as he tried to lean forward to kiss his mother's hand. She stopped him by pressing herself against his chest. He was as thin as a sickly child and she could almost lift him. "Come, my son, let's go in. You must be very hungry. Come, I'll take care of you. I won't let anyone harm you anymore. Come, my love, just a bit further, that's it, come. Easy, gentlemen, careful now! Can't you see how much pain he's in . . . ?"

The policemen struggled to carry Abel to the sitting room with Mina clinging to him. She refused to let her son go, worried he might vanish again. The men managed to get through the hallway, up the few steps, across the courtyard and into the sitting room. They deposited Abel on a mattress, but were shocked by his reaction. He flailed around, racked by shudders, and did all he could to hold on to the men, for fear the soft fabric might swallow him up. Twenty years of lying on concrete had taken its toll. Mina comforted him, wiped the sweat from his forehead with a handkerchief, and thanked the policemen. Before taking their leave, they clicked their heels and saluted the inert Abel as if he were a moribund general.

Mina had dreamed of this homecoming for so long that when it occurred she lost all her bearings. The ululating she'd dreamed of in her loneliest moments, the heartfelt shrieks she'd intended to unleash to proclaim her happiness to the world, gave way to silence and contemplation. She settled for holding her son's hand, without a single tear, without moaning. From time to time, Abel stroked her cheek and forgot to blink as he stared at the ceiling. Little smiles, glances, halting breaths, simple movements became their only interaction. Sensing that he was tired, Mina suggested that Abel stretch out as best he could and lay his head on her lap. He took care to avoid the spongy mattress. She ruffled his hair, as she had done many years before, in the days when she'd had sharp enough eyes to spot the lice the unruly lad brought home with him. She had spent hours patiently raking through the wild boy's thick mop of hair. Abel didn't object to his mother's tender combing, to the nimbleness of her fingers sending him into a deep sleep.

So my firstborn child had returned home, the boy I had publicly disowned.

We spent several days under the same roof without

seeing one another. Abel shut himself away in a room in the basement, crouched on the floor in the dark for hours. He couldn't stand light. Or noise. When Aïcha brought him his food he'd lower his head between his knees and shield his face as if he were about to be beaten. The elderly housemaid pretended not to notice, placed the tray in front of him and left the room as quickly as she could. "He still needs to escape that jail of his," she'd say to Mina, who stood worrying by the door. The two women comforted each other in the belief that time would help him heal. It was as though Mina had been granted another lease of life, and she took a new interest in running her home. As Abel no longer had any teeth to chew his favourite dishes, she cooked him soups: leak, Jerusalem artichoke, pumpkin and other seasonal vegetables. She made him purées of all kinds: beans, peas, aubergines with olive and *argan* oil. She had new ideas all the time. Sometimes she took him his food herself. She tiptoed into the room, placed the tray on the ground and sat next to him without saying a word or only whispered. She gradually got used to these quiet afternoons with her son. Total darkness brings benefits that normal-sighted people can't appreciate. Deprived of light, Mina felt the scope of her other senses. She learned to listen to her son's breathing, to interpret his almost soundless movements, to notice shifts in his soul, to read his thoughts, to gauge his moods. Despite appearances, Abel was not sad. He had achieved a point of stillness that was beyond the reach of most people. Mina intuited pretty quickly that to live in one's head, rather than in the glare of permanent exposure, provided a kind of freedom. Enough to make ordinary life seem dreary in comparison. One day she ventured to interrupt his silence with a question:

"Is this how you lived down there?"

Abel took a while to reply.

"In a way, but 'survived' would be a better way to describe it."

"Twenty years in complete darkness?"

"No, during the day you could more or less make out where the walls were."

"And the silence?"

"There's no such thing. If you stayed in this room with me for a few weeks you'd discover sounds you never imagined existed."

"So what did you hear in that place, my son?"

"A world of noises, Mother. The distant ticking of a windmill, the echoes of a call to prayer rising from the pits of the earth, a bird fleeing bad weather or a sand storm, an eerie chirping that heralded the death of a comrade. A whole world of noises, Mother, and if you were alert enough nothing escaped you. You could distinguish the scuttle of a cockroach from that of a scorpion."

Mina stared down at her feet in dismay. She couldn't see that Abel had guessed her reaction and smiled.

"Did you speak a lot with the others?"

"At the beginning, yes, because there were about thirty of us; the place was busy. The last few years things got quieter, of course. There were only four of us left."

"Where did everyone go?"

"They died. One by one, as the king wished."

Mina blew her nose. Her throat had tightened so much she couldn't speak.

"Drink a glass of water, Mother."

"You hate him, don't you?"

"The king? Not at all."

"But how's that possible?"

"It's a matter of survival, that's all."

She gave this some thought.

"Don't worry, my son, I have enough resentment for us all."

"I feel no hatred towards Papa either. In fact, I'd like to see him again."

"Are you sure?"

"Yes, I'm sure."

"You know . . ."

"Yes, I know."

"And you're not angry with him?"

"I'm not angry with anyone."

"But you do know that he . . ."

"He had no choice, Mother. And I've seen the havoc hatred leaves behind – I saw it in that death hole."

Mina blew her nose again.

"How can you feel no hatred towards those who brought so many tears to this house?"

Abel cleared his throat.

"Before harming others, hatred poisons the heart of those who harbour it, and it erodes and gnaws away at you, kills you, bit by bit."

"But how do you root it out of your heart when it has sunk so deep?"

"Forgiveness is a miracle. Of the thirty prisoners in the B block, only four of us survived, because we spat the poison of hatred out."

"Is it that easy to forgive your executioner?"

"There are no executioners, just people who administer the ordeals God has imposed on us."

"Why not have hatred for God then?"

"God is Love. I discovered that in jail."

One evening, Mina came and knocked on my bedroom door. I'd just had the most exhausting day as Sidi had been in an execrable mood.

"Come in," I said.

"Your son would like to see you."

"Let him in."

Mina ushered Abel in, pleased to see him walk without crutches. She closed the door and stood in the corridor, listening, fearful that an argument might break out. She heard nothing for a long time. Not a word, not a breath. Worried, she stuck her ear against the door.

After a drawn-out silence, when she seemed to have stopped breathing altogether, she heard the faint sound of two men crying.

13

SIDI WAS FINDING IT hard to walk. He paused after each step to catch his breath and lean on his stick – a treasured cane with an ivory handle carved into a roaring lion's head. I'd admired it for years. He used it for state occasions and liked to twirl it from side to side as he scoured the palace alleyways. But no longer. Now it had become a prop for his feeble body, a body so sick it was almost unable to move. His devastating insomnia had left him more drawn than ever. His saggy eyelids almost hid his pupils and unsightly bags drooped onto his cheekbones. Even though I'd often get home late, the chamberlain would summon me early the following morning. I regularly slept at the palace, too, for the sake of convenience. I loved to stroll alongside the king when the flames in his belly offered him a reprieve. It was only thanks to such moments of respite that Sidi kept going – and we would walk, shoulder to shoulder, like old friends. We barely spoke, just exchanged the odd word. I'd been my master's companion for so many years that I knew exactly, without a moment's hesitation, when I had to chip in.

That morning we sat on a bench in the shade of a flowering jacaranda tree.

"I love these purple flowers," he told me. "I have no idea why painters associate purple and violet with death."

"I agree, Sidi, there's nothing gloomy about these colours, but you know how artists are. They like to baffle people."

"Don't I know it! They're a race apart, sensitive souls, happy on the outside yet filled with pain inside, unbelievably touchy, too. They have colossal egos to boot. I've always felt very at home with them."

"That's why you kept me on, Your Majesty."

The king smiled.

"In ancient texts," I continued, "death is generally associated with a violent light, so blinding you can't make anything out. Colours only return once the doors of paradise have opened."

Sidi looked up at the cloudless sky and surveyed the tree scattered with flowers.

"This is the last time I'll see this blossoming tree, isn't it, Mohamed?"

Under normal circumstances I would have taken issue with this, certainly strongly denied it. I would have multiplied the time my master had left to live by a million. That was my task: I was paid to provide happiness, to come up with the words the king wanted to hear, to thread my illusions with pretty red ribbons and sell him eternity with a straight face. And he had to pretend to believe me.

Under normal circumstances, Sidi would have wanted to hear my lies, my far-fetched flattery, words drizzled with honey, as if spilling from a plentiful hive . . . but not that day. Neither of us wanted to cheat. Sidi expected me to treat him like a dying friend who had no more use for deception. My heart was pounding as I allowed myself to do something for which I could have been given a hundred lashes. Something no-one had ever dared do. I took my master's hand and held it very tight. A bony, wrinkled hand. He didn't pull away. He let it happen. We stayed like this, without a word, for a long while. Then he passed me his walking stick.

"Here, take it."

"It's your favourite cane, Sidi. I love to see you twiddle it about."

"I want you to have it."

I took it and ran my fingers over the handle, over the roaring lion's mane.

"It's beautiful."

"It belonged to my father."

"It should be given to the crown prince, not some old servant."

"You're not some old servant, Mohamed, you're my friend. I know you as well as you know me. You like this stick. Look after it."

He glanced up at the jacaranda tree.

"I won't see these flowers again, will I?"

I stared at his eyelids, hanging like drapes over his watery gaze.

"No, you won't see them again, Your Majesty."

MAHI BINEBINE is a Moroccan painter, sculptor and author, born in Marrakesh in 1959. He studied mathematics in Paris and taught the subject for eight years before returning to Morocco in 2002. He is the author of six novels, which have been translated into a dozen languages between them, and his paintings now form part of the permanent collection at the Guggenheim Museum in New York.

BEN FACCINI is a novelist, writer and translator. He is the author of several books, notably *The Water-Breather* (Flamingo, 2002) and *The Incomplete Husband* (Portobello, 2007), and is the translator of Lydie Salvayre's *Cry Mother Spain*.